MONSTERS
OUTTA MY HEAD

MONSTERS
OUTTA MY HEAD

D.R. Mills

SEA OF INK PRESS

MONSTERS
OUTTA MY HEAD

SEA OF INK PRESS

For my Dad.

I hope they have books up there for you, old man.

D.R. MILLS

PRESENTS . . .

PROLOGUE

Along the side of a paved road, a figure donned in a dark cloak walked toward a sleepy little mountain town. The sun rose overhead, bathing the star-filled sky with early morning light. The scent of wet pine permeated the air, and a thin fog settled over the pavement.

The figure raised his head. He looked forward with gleaming and bright yellow eyes resembling a cat's to see a large worn stone sign. Weeds curled and twisted up the sides, the untamed growth obscuring view. The letters carved deep into the stone said, *Welcome to Twilight Peak, Wyoming!* He'd arrived at last.

The figure's ears perked up at the piercing sound of tires screeching, and he turned to scan the road behind him. Blinding lights raced toward him. He sprinted into the nearby woods and leapt over a short barbed wire fence. Under the shade of the trees the figure prowled through vegetation, watching the road in anticipation as his heart pounded in his chest. *I'm so close*, he thought. *I can't get caught now... How did he catch up already?*

After a few moments, a rugged black truck stopped off the road, its large tires crunching over dirt and grass, light bars sloppily bolted to the top. In combination with the vehicle's headlights, brilliant beams sliced easily through the early morning fog. The driver's side door opened with an unnerving *creak* as the man behind the wheel climbed out and placed a dirty leather boot onto the ground.

The man looked younger, somewhere in his mid-twenties. Stubble covered his face. A large brimmed fedora-style hat sat atop his head, and shaggy brown hair escaped from underneath. He wore a T-shirt under a long black trench coat, his jeans riddled with various rips and stains.

The hooded figure watched, still as stone and quiet as death, while the man slammed his truck door and cast a suspicious glance at the treeline. Overhead, birds squawked, a gust of cold wind sweeping through the trees.

The man strolled closer to the barbed wire fence. He peered into the trees, carefully placing his hands between the barbs of the wire as his cold green eyes scanned the foliage for movement. The hooded figure remained perfectly still as the man gazed through the thick woods. Minutes passed, and finally the man smirked and turned away, then looked toward the town.

"Twilight Peak, huh…" he said, and climbed into his truck. He started it, the engine roaring to life. With a screech, the truck peeled onto the road, spewing rocks, dirt, and grass into the air behind.

The hooded figure watched the truck as it sped off. Once the vehicle was out of sight, he exited the treeline, staying low just in case. He took a deep breath and clutched the dagger at his hip with a hand covered in brown fur. The weapon had a smooth stone blade sharpened to a fine point and was tied to a handle made of bone with some old wire, hair, and small bits of tightly-woven rope.

He resumed his walk into town, the morning sun shining off the amulet hanging from his neck. With one hand on his dagger, and the other on his amulet, he journeyed onward, where he hoped his only friend in the world awaited his arrival.

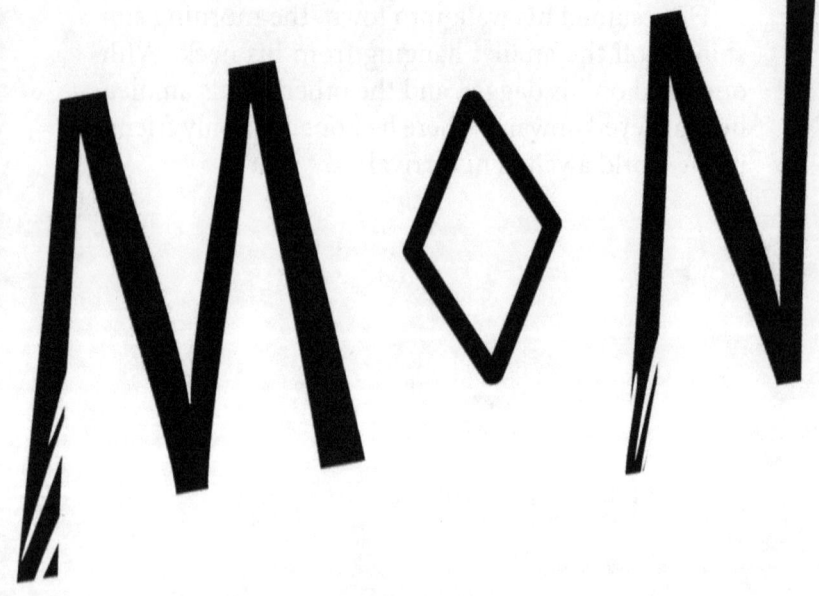

TERS

OUTTA

MY

HEAD

CHAPTER 1

"HELP ME! OH GOD, SOMEBODY
HELP ME, PLEASE!"

Fog and streams of light from the moon overhead swirled along the dark forest floor. The woman sprinted through its trees, scratching her legs on branches as she rushed past.

"Somebody, please!" she shouted, but her pleas fell unheard in the empty woods. The snarling beast behind her raced on all fours. Branches snapped against its hulking form as it charged forward.

She looked over her shoulder and screamed again. Her foot caught on the forest floor. She flew forward, then slammed into the ground, striking her head on something sharp. Pain shot through her skull. The grass *was cold and damp beneath her fingers, and her chest ached from exertion.*

A low growl sounded from behind. She rolled over, crying out. Glowing golden eyes burned into hers. A colossal beast with dirty and wild dark fur reared up on its hind legs and howled at the moon. The monster bared its teeth, each one splashed red with fresh blood.

She scrambled backward, but before she could escape, the beast overtook her with its massive body. Its breath filled her nostrils, the stench of rotten flesh assaulting her. The beast gnashed its fangs and bit into the soft skin of her--

Ryan bumped into another person just outside Mountain's Point High School. His book fell to the sidewalk and landed pages down. "Oh, sorry! I wasn't watching where I was…" He trailed off as he looked up to see a faded brown letterman jacket with yellow stripes. The figure in the jacket turned, and Ryan's chest tightened with dread.

"That's okay, creep. No harm, no foul," Todd Hallow, captain of the school's football team and its star quarterback, said with a sneer. His short black hair was unkempt, his hazel eyes filled with hostility.

Ryan avoided Todd's smug stare, his stomach churning as he nodded and leaned down to pick up his novel. Just as he grabbed the spine, Todd stepped on it, pinning it to the ground. "What's wrong, creep? Aren't you gonna pick up your book?" Ryan sighed and gave Todd a serious look, but Todd didn't budge. He only smirked. "I said, pick up your book, *creep*."

Ryan hesitated but leaned down to retrieve the item once more. Before he could grab it, Todd kicked him hard in the face. He stumbled to the right, into the dirt. Casually, Todd pushed the novel to the left with the side of his track shoe. It slid off the curb and splashed into a puddle.

Ryan groaned, his hands on his face as it throbbed with pain. All the while, Todd leaned over him. "Next time, watch where you're going, you little freak."

"Todd, step off," said the familiar voice of a girl. Ryan forced his eyes open to see Chyann Wakeman running toward them from the school building nearby. She stepped between them, but Todd only backed away slightly.

Chyann glared at Todd with green eyes. Bits of blonde streaked her mocha hair; her bangs hung just above her brow with the rest tied back in a ponytail. She wore jeans and a checkered plaid shirt, underneath a tank top sporting a bunny design. A necklace dangled from her throat, the heart pendant suspended from its chain shining silver and black.

Awe, c'mon, Ryan thought. *I don't wanna get pummeled by Todd again, but why is Chy always the one saving my ass?*

She dropped her backpack, stepping closer to Todd. "Leave him alone, or else."

Todd snorted. "Or else what? You gonna beat me up?"

"I could. You know I could. How would getting beat up by a girl feel on your ego?"

"When you gonna quit comin' to his rescue, huh?" Todd replied.

Chyann crossed her arms. "When you stop being a jerk. Now, I'm not gonna tell you again. Back off, or I call Willy down here. I'm sure he'd love to hear that you're out here slapping Ryan around. Especially after what happened *last time*."

Todd snorted once more. "The runt is in detention. Call all you want."

Chyann pulled out her cell phone. "You think that'll stop him?"

Todd hesitated to answer, as if silently debating whether he should continue. After a few moments of silence, he smiled a little. "One of these days, he's gonna piss me off, and you and the runt won't be around." He gave Ryan another smug look. "See you around, creep." With one final glare at Chyann, he turned and walked off toward the school building.

Once Todd was inside, Chyann turned to Ryan, offering a hand. "You okay, Ry?" He took her hand and climbed to his feet, brushing dirt off his light-blue zip up hoodie. She caressed his cheek, then looked his face over. "I don't think it'll bruise. Might be sore for an hour or two."

Ryan pulled away, ashamed Chyann had saved him once again. "I think I'm going to stop reading at school." He picked up his book from the puddle and looked it over. Dirty water stained the shine on the title's cover, *The Werewolf of the Darkwood*. As he opened it, wet pages tore and fell to pieces like cotton being pulled apart.

He closed his eyes. *Great, I just bought that yesterday. No way the 'warm spring air' is gonna save it either. Money well spent, I guess…* This wasn't the first time Todd had destroyed one of his possessions. He was sure it wouldn't be the last, either.

He opened his eyes and looked around, spotting a nearby trash can, then tossed the novel's remains inside.

Chyann gently patted him on the back as the two walked toward the main building. "He's such a jerk.

One of these days, I swear…"

"Forget him, Chy. He's just a bully."

"No kidding."

Ryan readjusted his bag, then gave Chyann a slight tap on the shoulder as she readjusted hers as well. "Thanks for having my back," he said, then continued with a hint of annoyance, "Again."

She smiled, tapping him in the same manner. "Hey, it's gonna happen whether you want it to or not. It would kinda be going against our whole 'three musketeers' thing if I just let Todd walk all over you."

Ryan forced a weak smile, hoping she would drop the topic. *That's Chy for you*, he thought. *Considering we've known each other since we were born, I guess it shouldn't surprise me anymore with how protective she is.*

Ryan brushed more dirt from his cropped black hair as he and Chyann entered the school, the familiar sounds of bustling students in the air. The walls were a dark red-and-orange series of bricks, the linoleum floors shiny and freshly waxed. Yellow and brown patterned lockers lined the hallways, along with various posters and papers which advertised all manner of after-school activities and events.

Ryan and Chyann turned left into one of the building's long halls, passing dozens of students. "Speaking of the three musketeers," Ryan began, "Is Will seriously in detention again?"

They approached Chyann's locker and she opened it. She gave Ryan a nod as she sorted through the contents inside, then stuffed some books into her backpack. "Yeah, he is."

"What did he do this time?"

"What do you think?" She closed her locker, and

the two walked through a chattering crowd and down the hall. "He's being Willy."

Mrs. Johnson was a stout middle-aged woman with graying hair and thick glasses resting on the end of her witch-like nose. She sat at a large table at the front of the classroom as golden rays streaked in from the windows, shining over rows of desks.

The only student here was Willy. He sat at the front desk, only a few feet away from Mrs. Johnson, completely bored out of his mind. He scratched his side-shave, trying not to fall asleep, then ran a hand through the most hair he had--a dark mohawk. He yawned, adjusting the collar of his ragged sweatshirt before looking down at his denim pants to ensure his fly wasn't unzipped from a previous trip to the bathroom.

He hit his fingers against the wood of his desk, his face turned toward the closest window. He glanced at the teacher. She looked up from her work and gave him an agitated stare.

After several sets of taps, she lowered her pen. "Stop that."

At this, a smile spread across Willy's face. *Jackpot.* He began tapping harder on the desk, and Mrs. Johnson leaned forward, narrowing her eyes at him as though silently demanding him to stop. Willy met her gaze, pausing momentarily before tapping once more.

The teacher took a long, angry breath. She set her pen down, then removed her glasses. "Willy, do you plan on spending the remainder of your eleventh grade year in detention?"

"That depends. Do you think you've got the patience to put up with me and my hilarious jokes for that long?"

"I have better things to do than sit here every morning and babysit you."

"What a coincidence. I have better things to do than sit here every morning and be babysat. I'm glad we got it sorted out."

Her sour stare didn't budge, but she said nothing. Just as she finally opened her mouth, Willy jumped from his seat on cue with the bell. "On that note"--he gave her a sly wink before heading for the door--"I'm a free bird once again. Don't worry, though. I'm sure I'll be back to keep you company within the hour."

He stepped out of the room and walked up to Ryan and Chyann, who waited across the hall for him, as per usual. They headed toward class.

"How was detention?" Chyann asked. Willy looked over his shoulder, back toward the classroom, and saw Mrs. Johnson as she rubbed her temples in frustration.

Willy offered Chyann his jolliest grin. "I think she likes me."

Lunch time finally rolled around, and amidst a crowd of fellow students Ryan, Chyann, and Willy entered the cafeteria. It was a large area with a tall ceiling, round tables with attached seats scattered about the floor. Students stood in a line leading to a smaller, separate room where they picked up their food. *At least lunch today is something edible*, Ryan thought.

After grabbing pizza and veggies, the trio walked to their everyday table, located in a corner far from everyone else.

"Why does Biology suck so much?" Willy whined. He took his seat and began to shovel food down his throat.

"Biology is pretty interesting, Will," Chyann replied. "Maybe if you'd pay attention once in a while, you wouldn't have such a hard time in there."

Willy swallowed his bite, dropped his head to his chest, and closed his eyes, then began snoring louder than a revving muscle car. A few seconds later, his eyes shot open and he returned to a sitting position. "Nerd," he said, grinning. Chyann replied with an unimpressed head shake.

Ryan pulled a binder from his backpack and placed it on the table next to his tray. "Thankfully we have English next, and I finished my report."

Chyann and Willy perked up at his comment, turning toward him. "It's about your grandpa, right?" Chyann asked.

"Yeah, it is. I stayed up all night trying to get it just right. Here, let me show you." He pulled out the paper and slid it toward her. "What do you think?" Chyann picked it up and began reading.

Willy wiped his mouth. "It's been a year already, hasn't it?"

Ryan frowned, his heart aching at the memory of his grandpa. "Yeah… a whole twelve months ago today. I still can't believe he's actually gone. He was a tough old guy. Kinda seemed like he was never gonna die, you know?"

"Oh trust me, I know," Willy said. "I still don't understand how he was in his late seventies and moved like he was thirty."

Ryan chuckled. Hot tears welled in his eyes, but he forced them back. "Yeah…" He shook his head. "He always said he had to stay in shape if he wanted to keep up with all the elk."

Chyann handed the report to Ryan with a sad smile. "It's great, Ry. He'd love it."

"Thanks." He tucked it into his binder.

"Are you sure you're okay to do this?" she asked. "I know he's a sensitive subject."

Ryan wiped his eyes, determined to stay strong this time. "Yeah, I'm sure. I feel good about it. Like, if I share what was so great about him, it'll help ease some of the pain, y'know?" Chyann and Willy nodded. "It's gonna be great." Ryan closed his binder.

Ryan and Chyann began eating their lunch. As casual conversation took over, he glanced across the cafeteria to see Todd as the bully sneered at them, his fellow tablemates following his gaze with similar expressions as they continued their own discussions.

Willy sat at a desk in his English classroom, his eyes heavy as he watched Chyann give her presentation at the front of the large open space.

Desks were settled in neat rows atop the tiled floor, and Willy pulled uncomfortably at the collar of his gray sweater. Despite the size of the room, the air felt so hot and stuffy he thought it might choke him to death, sweat already forming on his chest and in his armpits.

This school sucks, Willy thought. *Somebody take me out back and shoot me. As much as I hate home, at least it's got air conditioning.*

Finally, Chyann neared the end of her report. "In conclusion, my mother is a great influence on me because every day she manages to teach me something new. Thank you." Together, Willy and Ryan offered her a thumbs up. The rest of the class launched into slightly enthusiastic applause, and Chyann took a bow, then returned to her seat.

Ms. Davis stood from her desk and adjusted her glasses and fuzzy mahogany-colored vest. "All right class, who would like to present next?" The room went silent. Ms. Davis glanced over face after face, and soon her gaze locked on Willy. "What about you, Willy? Is your report ready to share?"

Willy leaned forward with a grin. "Right, so, funny story. I--"

"Is this a story regarding an inspirational family member?"

"There's… a good chance it's not." The laughter of students filled the room.

Ms. Davis nodded as if she were unsurprised and disappointed all the same. She returned her attention to the rest of the class. "Anybody else?"

The room fell silent once again. Only seconds passed before her attention fell on Ryan. "What about you, Ryan?"

The class turned to him, including the prick Todd, who sat at the back of the classroom, and Willy faced his friend, trying to offer the boy quiet encouragement. *Knock 'em dead, bro. You got this.*

The pale, black-haired boy stood. A shaky breath escaped his lips, and the pink of his cheeks drained away as he headed to the front of the classroom. Once he got there he held up his report, cleared his throat, and began to read. "When I was little, my grandfather used to tell me all kinds of scary stories. Sometimes I would sit with him for hours while he told me tale after tale about supernatural creatures. On rare occasions, he would even ramble on about his own experiences with the paranormal. He always used to tell me, 'This town isn't as boring as you may think.' I never knew what he meant by that, but--"

"Oh my God," Todd blurted from the back. "Do you ever talk about anything else?" The class turned to Todd. "Like anybody wants to listen to him yap about ghosts and werewolves and all that crap. *Again.*"

Ms. Davis stood. "Todd, you can either apologize and be quiet, or head to the office. We need to have respect for the speaker when he or she presents."

"Why should I? It's not like I'm the only one thinking it."

"Shut it, Todd," Chyann yelled.

Todd rolled his eyes. "There you go, standing up for him again."

"Of course I'm gonna," Chyann retorted. "He's my best friend."

The class began laughing and whispering. Willy looked to Ryan, who stood frozen at the front of the room. His expression was still, emotionless, but his brown eyes began to glisten under the overhead lights.

Ms. Davis crossed her arms and opened her mouth, but before she could say a word, Todd cut her off. "I don't care how close you guys are," Todd said. "The bottom line is that kid is a freak." Willy swung around to glare at Todd, but Todd wouldn't meet his gaze; the bully only stared at Ryan, venom on his lips. "A major *freak*."

Willy ground his teeth, nostrils flaring. All focus shifted to Ryan. *Come on, man. Tell Todd to shove it. Tell the guy something.*

Without a word, Ryan slammed his report onto the teacher's desk, grabbed his backpack, and left the classroom.

Attention fell to Todd. Some students laughed while others remained quiet. Ms. Davis scowled at them.

Willy fell back in his chair, jaw clenched. *All right, that's it. Maybe Ry's cool with letting Todd say crap like this, but I'm not.*

Willy rose to face the bully. "Why don't you shut your face, jockstrap?"

Todd glowered at Willy before finally his signature smirk returned. Most of the kids talking went silent, but some made "ooo" sounds, as though they knew that Willy's standing up was going to lead to something big.

"What did you just say to me, runt?" Todd snarled.

"Oh, my bad. I forgot that you're not just stupid, you're also deaf. I said shut your face, jockstrap."

Todd flipped his desk and lunged. Willy refused to budge, unafraid.

"*Boys!*" Ms. Davis shouted. Todd shoved Willy with his chest. Despite the clear full foot height difference between them, Willy remained undaunted, shooting daggers into the bully.

"You gonna beat me up?" Todd teased.

Willy slid his hands into his sweatshirt pocket. "I'll do worse than that." He glanced at Ms. Davis and winked. "Off school grounds, of course. Wouldn't wanna get detention."

"Boys, that's enough," the teacher said, but it fell on deaf ears. Todd shoved Willy with burly hands. Willy stumbled backward, slamming his ankle into the metal of a nearby desk. A feeling like heavy static shot up his leg.

Finally, Ms. Davis stepped between them. "I said that's enough! Todd, to principal Bullworth's office right now, and don't drag your feet."

Todd glared at her, his mouth twitching. He turned to leave the class. "This isn't over, runt."

"What are you, a freakin' Saturday morning cartoon villain?" Willy retorted.

The teacher turned to him as Todd left. "Sit down and stay quiet unless you want to go, too."

Chyann hopped to her feet and grabbed Willy's hand, then pulled him back into his seat. "C'mon, Will. He's not someone worth getting expelled over."

Willy said nothing, and the class sat unmoving. Quiet conversation trickled through the air as Ms. Davis walked to her desk. Once she reached it, she began to dial on her classroom phone, presumably to call the office.

One of these days… Willy thought.

As the tension in the room began to die down, so did Willy's anger, replaced with a hollow pit deep in his stomach. He gazed at Chyann. The shine in her eyes was dimmed, her brow knit as she stared sadly at Ryan's empty chair.

Class continued, but it was all just background noise now. *What's that roid-monkey's problem, anyway?* Willy struggled to find an answer. As far back as he could remember, Todd had always bullied Ryan, and many students followed the bully's lead. It was funny how one popular kid shouting the words weird, creep, or loser somehow made it gospel for the rest to preach.

Who needs 'em, anyway? They might all be a bunch'a sheep, but at least they know I can beat his ass.

Willy was fairly certain most of the kids their age knew that if it came down to Willy fighting Todd, Willy would probably win. He had made half his reputation around school by fighting, and usually winning, against kids like Todd. *If Ms. Davis wasn't here, he would'a been eating through a straw by now.*

He patted his pant pocket, suddenly remembering his Swiss army knife. He'd used it countless times over the years to carve initials into many desks with the blade. He thought briefly about using it against Todd, but quickly decided against it. *I don't need a knife to turn his mouth inside out. All I need is one good...*

A flash of movement in his peripheral vision derailed his train of thought, and he realized Chyann was waving at him. Her eyes were stern and she shook her head, almost like she was going to say, "*No Will, he's not worth getting in big trouble over, no matter how much he deserves it.*"

She'd said this countless times, and she was right.

He hated when she was, which of course was all the freakin' time. It drove him crazy.

He gave her an eye roll and she turned around to face the front of the classroom. *All right. Have it your way, Chy. I won't beat Todd up. No matter how much he freakin' deserves it.*

CHAPTER 2

Ryan swung the door open and wandered into his room, phone to his ear. He tossed his backpack onto the carpeted floor. "No, Chy. I'm not coming back."

He made his way from one end to the other in just a few strides, passing his medium-sized TV and the tall bookshelf pushed up against his far wall. The shelf held many books on supernatural myths, legends, and the occult, plus various horror stories by an array of authors.

"Please?" Chyann pleaded on the other end of the call. "You can't keep letting Todd push you around like this."

"No, I'm not coming back. Not for the rest of the day."

She sighed. "Are you sure?"

"I'm sure. Think I'm just gonna stay at home this afternoon. Catch up on some homework."

"Well, all right. We'll come over after school and do something, okay?"

Ryan collapsed onto his bed. "Sounds good. Later." He hung up, then dropped his phone atop the pillow near his head.

He lay there a moment, staring at the ceiling, his stomach clenching. *I should have known better than to discuss something so personal within earshot of Todd.*

Anything and everything he had ever brought up around Todd had been met with either a fate similar to his book that morning, or had just been outright ridiculed. Nothing seemed to be safe from that guy's wrath.

But there's nothing I can do about it, he thought. Averagely built, and only a little more physically fit than someone who didn't take part in any sport or gym membership, he wasn't much of a threat to someone like Todd. The bully was as muscular as you would expect an athlete to be, with the quarterback prowess to boot. If Ryan tried to stand up to the guy, there was no doubt in his mind he'd get beaten to a bloody pulp.

His only option was to take the abuse, walk away, and hope he didn't get sent to the nurse's office again. That was what he was supposed to do anyway, right? As far as the teachers were concerned at least. He had told countless school staff about his suffering at the hands of the star quarterback, but nothing ever seemed to change. Bully or not, it seemed they cared more for their image on the football field than the harassment of a single student.

Ryan looked over at a framed picture on his bedside table. The photo was taken on a lakeside, featuring himself, his mother, and his grandfather Magnus. Each of them smiled wide, holding up their own large fish. Ryan reached over and took the picture in his hand. His mother looked so beautiful here, with short blonde hair, soft features, and a straight smile. His grandfather had a strong yet gentle face, spiderwebs of wrinkles etched into his sun-kissed skin. He had no hair here, but Ryan had never known him to anyway, since the old man had always preferred to be bald.

Ryan stared at the picture, memories of the day filling his head: summer rays shining down on them, the fresh air of the lake, and all of the laughter and joy.

When grandpa was still alive, he'd always made sure to take the family on trips like that every other weekend so long as the weather allowed. "We only have so much time on this earth together," he'd said. "So let's be sure we make the most of it."

Ryan's smile melted away, his grip tightening on the sides of the frame. Hot tears welled in the corners of his vision as he focused on his grandfather's face.

There weren't going to be any more family trips like that. There hadn't been since grandpa died.

Ryan missed those days. It wasn't fair how much life had changed since grandpa's death. Grandpa had taught him so much, and ever since the old man passed, he felt as though he were lost in a winding maze. Not to mention his mother had thrown herself into her work as a nurse since the event, which had left him mostly to his own devices.

A loud *pop* sounded from outside. Ryan snapped

out of his thoughts and jumped to his feet. He set the frame onto his bedside table, peering through his window.

The street outside was paved with decades-old cement. Cracks riddled the surface, weeds growing rampant from every crevice. Dust swirled and danced across the rocky surface in the afternoon breeze. Just beyond the street stood an endless stretch of oak trees, an area of thick wood Ryan and his friends had always called the Witch's Woods.

Moments of searching went by before he gave up. *Maybe it was just a tire blowing out in the street or something.* That seemed a fair explanation, as people often tossed glass bottles and other hazardous trash out of their windows as they drove by.

Just as he turned away from the window, movement caught his eye. He swung around. A hooded figure darted into the brush, there and gone before he could get a good look.

A second later, a man in a dark hat and coat ran in the same direction as the hooded figure, and Ryan narrowed his eyes, confused. As the man moved, something silver gleamed in his grip.

The man in the dark hat and coat disappeared into the Witch's Woods, and another loud *pop* sounded in the air.

What the hell was that? Is somebody... His heart pounded against his ribcage as realization set in. The sounds were *gunshots.*

He backed away, his mind racing with questions. *Who were those guys? Why are they shooting a gun?* He turned toward his desk. A large pocket knife sat there, next to his laptop and textbooks. *What should I do?*

He stared at the weapon for a moment, his hands growing slippery with sweat, before turning to his phone on the bed.

The cops. Call the cops. That's what grandpa would do, right?

Another gunshot echoed in the distance, and he glanced through the window once more.

△

Ryan flipped out the blade of his pocket knife and turned it over in his hands as he ran through the brush.

Every fiber of his being screamed at him to turn back, to call the police, but something else, something deep within his gut, called out to investigate the matter himself.

His jacket billowed behind him as he sprinted under rows of tall oak trees. He stumbled over a root sticking out from the ground but managed to maintain his balance, then continued forward.

The woods suddenly went silent and he slowed to a stop, looking around, unsure of where to go next. All those times he'd hunted with his grandfather had given him a fair level of skill in tracking, so he just needed a sign of some kind: a broken twig, disturbed vegetation, *something*.

He carefully scanned the area around, and his gaze eventually stopped on a nearby bush. Branches were freshly snapped off, which showed a clear sign that somebody had recently rushed through it with enough force to break the thin limbs rather than bend them. He tiptoed toward the bush, ready to investigate further.

Another gunshot blasted through the air, and the birds overhead squawked. Shock reverberated through Ryan's body like a current, his breath catching in his throat. *That sounded* very *close.* He tightened his grip on the pocket knife, steeling his nerves, then ran toward the echoes.

Minutes passed, and finally he came to a halt and peered through the trees. He kneeled. His chest burned hotter than fire from all the exertion, but thankfully some shade from the trees above covered him, keeping him hidden as he stared ahead into a small clearing.

The man in the trench coat stood alone in the glade, glancing around with a suspicious look in his eyes. His shaggy dark brown hair jutted out from under his hat as if he hadn't brushed it in some time, and stubble covered his face, a small pencil-line scar set just under the right corner of his mouth. He wore dirty black combat boots, ripped and faded jeans tucked into the tightly tied shoes.

In his right hand, the man clutched a silver colt revolver with a sturdy whitewood handle, a large "**H**" carved into the wood. He held the gun high above his head as he slowly paced the clearing.

"Here kitty, kitty, kitty..." the man hummed, a smug grin plastered on his lips. "You can't run from me forever!"

The hooded figure--the same one Ryan saw earlier--rose swiftly from the brush behind the gunman and struck with a dagger.

The man in the trenchcoat turned, but the dagger caught his arm. The blade tore through his jacket sleeve and he dropped his colt revolver, stumbling backward. Ryan gasped as he watched, free hand over his mouth. He squinted at the hooded figure, trying to make out any features to further identify, but their face was swathed in complete darkness beneath the cloak.

"A foolish death is fitting only for a fool," the deep and menacing voice of a man said. Ryan guessed the voice belonged to that of the hooded figure, as it sounded nothing like the man in the trench coat.

The hooded man readjusted his grip on the knife and lunged for the man in the coat, but his opponent ducked and swiftly stepped behind him. He snarled, whirling around and catching his enemy by the neck from behind.

"And now you're going to die for your foolishness," the hooded man began, pressing his blade against his opponent's throat, "For every life you've taken."

The man in the trench coat smiled. "Took the words right outta my mouth." He swung his head backward. It slammed against his adversary's still-concealed face.

The man in the coat lumbered ahead to freedom while the hooded man stumbled to the side, his cloak falling down to reveal his face. Ryan caught a glimpse of the man, finally able to identify his appearance, but nearly cried out at the realization that he couldn't be human at all.

Well actually, upon closer inspection, maybe he was a *little* human, but he had to be mixed with something else. And, from the looks of it, that something else was probably a cat. Instead of skin, brown fur with orange stripes covered him, small pointed ears pricked up on either side of his head. His feline eyes shone bright yellow, and blood trickled out from his perfect pink triangle of a nose located in the middle of his face. Whiskers twitched just above his top lip, while a pair of short fangs protruded out from under it.

I can't believe what I'm seeing, Ryan thought, swallowing hard. *That's gotta be some kind of costume, right?*

The man in the trench coat gathered his composure. He fixed his hat, snatched up his gun, and turned to the cat-man. The creature wiped the blood from his face with one fur-covered arm and glared at his enemy.

It can't be a costume, no. Looks too real. And why are they trying to hurt each other, anyway?

The gunman aimed his colt revolver and pulled the hammer back with a smile. "I know what you're thinking, 'Did he shoot five bullets, or six?'" He tilted his head. "So how about it, Boss? Feelin' lucky?"

They stood in silence for almost a minute before Boss tightened his grip on the dagger and rushed forward, a flash of movement. He stabbed at the man, missed, followed it up with a quick hack. But the man dodged the attacks with ease, smiling still.

However, Boss wouldn't give up. He extended sharp claws from the tips of his free hand and struck the man with them, followed by a quick stab of the dagger, barely swiping the man's chest.

The man sneered, catching the creature's arm, then fired a single round into his adversary's chest. Ryan shrank back, his ears ringing with shrill echoes.

Boss choked. Blood flew from his mouth and he

collapsed onto his back, onto the ground. His dagger tumbled aside.

The man in the coat smiled and blew the smoke from his barrel. "Guess it just wasn't your lucky day." He strolled around the cat creature, his expression morphing into that of glee, and Ryan watched with wide eyes, his heart beating like a rhythmic drum. He tightened his sweat-soaked hands around the handle of his pocket knife.

"It's been almost two years of this little cat and mouse shit," the man said in an accomplished tone. He stopped and looked down at the writhing creature. "Well, cat and *man*."

Boss grimaced and reached inside his cloak, then pulled out a metal chain with a gold-and-silver amulet hanging from it. Strange symbols were carved into the talisman, a glittering scarlet gem mounted in its very center.

The man in the trench coat knit his eyebrows at the item and, despite the blood leaking from Boss's mouth and seeping from the wound in his chest, the cat-man raised the amulet and spoke.

"**Custódi ánimam meam, et transferre ad alium autem infirma…**" The man backed away as the crystal began to glow, and its light grew in intensity as the creature continued, "**Et animam meam de novo!**"

The gem flashed three times, radiant red rays blinding Ryan. He quickly covered his eyes and turned away.

When the light finally faded, Ryan swung around to peer into the clearing once more, to watch what Boss had done. *What the hell is happening?*

Now the scarlet beams shone not only from the

amulet, but they also came from Boss's eyes. The yellow in his stare was gone, replaced with the same red of the talisman's crystal, glowing bright.

Boss glared at the man in the trench coat. "**Et nunc tu es.**" The amulet glistened again, and the cat creature's eyes did the same.

Moments passed, and finally Boss let out a strained breath, then fell limp and lifeless, dropping his talisman. The object tumbled into the dirt, and as its luminosity began to dim, so did the shine in his feline stare.

Did... that guy just kill him? Ryan thought. He blinked hard, examining the scene, his gaze traveling over to the cat creature's open cloak, where a key on a string tied around his neck lay against his unmoving, fur-covered chest. He appeared void, no semblance of a soul inside.

The man in the trench coat stood dumbfounded before raising a hand to his chin. "What the hell was that all about?" he blurted, and Ryan wondered the same thing.

Suddenly a strange, dreadful sensation--something terrifying yet unexplainable, something that pulled at the core of Ryan's being--came over him, the hairs on his arms and neck standing on end. A sharp ticking sounded in his ears, and his stomach tied itself in knots. Then a new voice, the unfamiliar and deep voice of an old man, whispered from behind, "It's time, my boy. Time to accept your destiny."

Panic jolted through Ryan, and he jumped to his feet and spun around, knife ready. However, the green woods were clear behind him, no sign of anybody having been there. Ryan briefly wondered if he had heard a voice at all. Today in general was beginning to feel like a nightmare.

Scarlet light flashed in his peripheral. He spun around, toward the clearing, to see the man in the coat as he threw up his arms and backed away from the amulet, which seemed to be a fair enough reaction, since now the talisman thrummed against the ground, vibrating as though an energy was building from inside of it.

The amulet fired a red beam of light into the brush, straight for Ryan. But before he could even do so much as scream, it speared him through the chest.

The force knocked him off his feet and sent him rolling backward, his entire body going numb before static started buzzing through each of his limbs. He hit his head on something hard and came to a stop.

Ryan groaned. His vision spun, his head throbbing with pain, static whizzing behind his eyes. *What the hell?* He blinked several times, trying to get rid of the blurriness, then sat up and looked around. The hurt behind his eyes was intense. He felt as though he'd been hit by a truck.

There was an old oak behind him, still standing tall, which he guessed was probably the culprit behind his headache. His pocket knife lay nearby, buried in the lush grass. He snatched it up, then held it at the ready as another man's voice--no, it wasn't just any regular man, it sounded like the cat creature's voice, the one he was pretty sure he'd just watched die--rang through his mind like a bell in a small locked room: *"Unless you want to die, I suggest you stay silent. Do not utter a word, no matter how startling my presence may be, and leave this area. Quickly."*

"*Obviously I need to get out of here,*" Ryan thought, partly in response to the voice, partly to himself. "*But what just happened? What's going on?*"

As if in reply, a red glow flashed before him, and chills bolted down his spine. Smoke gathered in the corners of his vision, curling and twisting until it formed a transparent and ghostly visage. Within moments the phantom shifted into a deep brown color, then morphed into one half of a face, the face of the cat creature named Boss, which now hovered over the left side of Ryan's own face like an incomplete mask.

Boss's visible eye gleamed yellow. The cat creature looked ahead, toward the clearing. "*There's no time to answer your questions right now,*" he replied, his voice still ringing from inside Ryan's mind. "*You must do as I say, or the both of us will die. Now stay low, remain quiet, and leave.*"

Ryan sat, dumbfounded, wide eyes locked on the apparition of the cat-man before him. He opened and closed his mouth repeatedly, so many questions swarming his brain he couldn't form a reply, until finally he did something he probably shouldn't have.

He screamed and stumbled backward, into the tree behind. The blood pumping in his ears nearly drowned out all other sounds.

Boss snarled. "*I said to stay* quiet!"

Footsteps bounded toward them, and Ryan turned to see the man in the trench coat stomp through the brush. He took one look at Ryan, at the cat creature hovering above the boy's face, and smiled in surprise, like a child opening an unexpected Christmas present.

"Well, how about that?" The man chuckled as he spoke, stepping closer. "That was some lightshow you put on back there, Whiskers"--he wagged his index finger--"but you're not getting off that easy. Trying to possess some poor kid, too?"

Boss frowned. "If it's any consolation, I was aiming for you." This time his voice wasn't just coming from inside Ryan's head, though. It sounded outside as well, and Ryan assumed Boss did this so the man could hear everything the cat creature uttered.

The man's grin widened, and he shifted his attention from Boss to Ryan. "How old are you, kid?" Only a hint of concern laced his tone.

"I'm, uhhh, s-seventeen," Ryan stuttered.

The man shook his head. "And this monster has used his magic to enter your body?" Ryan scrunched his nose, and the man laughed and spoke again. "Sorry, phrasing." *He sure is awfully calm about all of this...*

The man continued, almost sadly, "Life sure ain't fair, is it?" He grabbed Ryan's arm and pulled the boy up with ease.

Ryan craned his neck back slightly, his breathing growing shallow. "You can reverse this, right?" His voice cracked as he asked the question.

The man's relaxed smile faded, and his expression changed into something else. Something sinister. "I don't think so. Sorry, kid." He raised his colt revolver, and Ryan froze. "I'm gonna have to put you down to put the cat down. Think of it as a, ummm..." He thought for a moment, then shrugged. "Think of it as a 'hero's sacrifice,' or something. It's for the greater good."

"B-b-but there's-- There's gotta be something you can do to split us back up again!"

"If there is, only he would know," the man replied,

then pulled the hammer of the colt back and pressed its barrel against Ryan's forehead, the steel like ice on his clammy skin.

"So what'll it be, Boss?" the man asked as the cat creature glowered at him. "You gonna save the kid and tell me how to reverse your little spell, or are you gonna take him down with you? You know, this isn't an easy choice for me, either."

Deafening silence settled between them and then, without a word, Boss's face faded away, leaving behind only a few tendrils of curling smoke.

Ryan's breath caught in his throat, and the man smirked. "So be it then. Sorry, kid. Better luck next time, huh?" He pulled the trigger. The gun clicked, out of ammunition. His face dropped.

Ryan gathered his composure. He tightened his grip on the pocket knife and stabbed with a yell. The blade pierced the man's shoulder. He screeched, releasing Ryan.

The man pressed a hand to his wounded shoulder, and Ryan yanked out the blade and stumbled backward. The man lurched back as well. He tripped over an exposed root and fell to the ground, then removed his hand from his shoulder, liquid crimson splashed across his palm. He turned to Ryan, nostrils flaring.

"Run, you fool!" Boss's voice echoed through Ryan's mind once again. The boy swung around and sprinted into the trees with furious speed.

"Get back here *you little brat*!" the man screamed. The hollers chased after Ryan as he ran, ducking under low hanging branches that grabbed at him like sinister claws. He shoved them away, and one snagged his jacket sleeve. *No*, he thought. *I don't have time for this!* He tugged hard and the branch snapped, freeing him.

From behind, the man's furious shrieks were still audible. "Don't think you can hide from me!"

Ryan kept running, heart pounding in his chest, until he'd escaped the Witch's Woods and reached the street in front of his home. He dashed between his house and the neighbors', then hastened into the alleyway behind. *Gotta head around back. If he sees me go in through the front door, I'm a goner.*

He rushed alongside his backyard fence, toward an old chained-up gate and then, without error, squeezed under the links and through the barrier. Chest burning, he ran to the back door nearby, the one leading to his garage, and yanked it open so hard he thought he might tear it from its hinges. As he rushed inside, he pulled it shut behind him, then hurried toward the other door in his garage, the one leading out to the front of his home.

He gasped for breath, his legs sore and unbalanced from the unexpected exercise. Once he'd somewhat recuperated, he pressed his cheek against the door's tiny window, its glass warm to the touch from the afternoon sun, and watched for his assailant.

The man sprinted out from the vegetation across the street, looking around with an expression so angry Ryan could practically see steam coming from his ears. Soon it appeared the man was yelling at the whole neighborhood. He shook his head and pumped his fists, and although Ryan wasn't quite sure what the man said next, he had a pretty fair idea it wasn't family friendly.

Police sirens wailed in the distance and, with each passing moment, grew closer. The man took one last frantic glance in their direction before stomping his foot and heading back into the woods.

Finally safe at home, Ryan sighed in relief. He hurried into the house, then moved through the kitchen and down the hall toward his room. He slammed the door shut, taking shaky breaths as he struggled to calm himself.

He gazed down at his shaking hand that still clutched the pocket knife. Both his skin and the blade were covered with droplets of blood. He tossed the weapon into the garbage can by his door, then backed away, toward his bed. *I'm gonna be sick.* Questions raced through his thoughts in rapid succession.

Who were those guys?

What were they even doing out there?

Why didn't I just stay here and call the cops?

Ryan flinched as a flash of red appeared just outside the edges of his vision. *Oh God, not again.*

Tendrils of smoke formed, taking shape into the left half of Boss's face, settling itself over Ryan. "Compose yourself, child," Boss said. "He's gone, but he will be back. He'll be looking for me."

Ryan stared at Boss's ghostly half-face in disbelief, unsure of what to say, his breaths coming in quick gasps. After a few moments, he finally managed to choke out a reply. "W-what are you?"

"I'm an Ooawan. But, well, I suppose humans might call me something like a... hmmm. Perhaps 'monster cat' would be the correct phrasing?"

"But that's impossible."

Boss huffed. "And yet, here we are."

"What is this exactly? Are you like, possessing me? Like that guy said?"

"No, I'm..." He fell silent for a few seconds. "To

be honest, I'm not sure what this is. I think I'm more just... how would you say it?"

"Uhh, riding shotgun?"

Boss looked down with his one visible eye, his nose scrunched up ever so slightly. "Aye, I suppose that's one way you could describe it."

Ryan stumbled back. He fell against his bedside and slid into a seated position, sweat collecting on his forehead. However, whether it was from all the running or from everything else that was happening, he couldn't be sure. His entire body ached, but not like it would from a bit of sprinting. This pain was something different, and Ryan had a sinking feeling it was because of Boss's magic. At least the intense sensation behind his eyes from earlier had subsided.

They sat in silence for a while before Boss lowered his gaze. "I'm sorry."

"For what?"

"For dragging you into this. You were nearly killed."

Ryan mulled the apology over, then took a few deep breaths. "So how exactly do we, you know, put you back in your own body?"

"I'm not entirely sure I *can* be put back."

Ryan laughed coldly, his eyes growing watery. "Right. Of course. That's just... that's great."

"Look, this isn't exactly ideal for me either."

"But if you were trying to possess the other guy, then why'd you have to move in with me instead, huh?" Ryan balled his fists. "Maybe you don't know how to use that spell or whatever it was as well as you think you do."

Boss narrowed his visible eye. "I performed the action perfectly. You must have been closer to me than he was. And it was an *amulet*, not a spell. To perform spells you must be a witch or some other higher…" He trailed off, his gaze drifting away as if he were thinking about something.

"Oh, so sorry," Ryan said, throwing his hands in the air. "It was a magical amulet instead of a spell. My bad!"

The Ooawan didn't respond, Ryan's sarcasm lost on him, until finally something like a smile tugged on his catlike mouth. "The amulet, that's it! It's used to perform the magic, so perhaps it can undo it."

"Are you sure?"

"No, but we must try. After all, would you rather we remain trapped together like this?"

Ryan ran his hands through his hair and groaned. "So what now, then? Do we go grab your body? 'Cause we can't go out there, not with the cops and the crazy guy with the gun stomping around in the woods."

"I doubt my body will still be there. He probably took it with him, the mad man…"

A few thoughts about what the man might do with Boss's corpse crossed Ryan's mind, and his stomach turned. "Why would he want it?"

"Because as careless as he is, he wouldn't leave my remains lying around for anybody to come across. He's been raised not to leave evidence behind."

Ryan shook his head. This was all too much to handle. "Who the hell is this guy anyway? Why does he want to kill you?"

"His name is Steven Van Helsing, and he wants me dead because he and his family think that my kind are violent. He believes we pose a threat to humanity."

"Uh, do you?"

"No, of course not. We were peaceful. We lived

in the mountains, in thick woods, far away from humans. Very few of your kind knew about us and where we lived. And now because of him, my village has been destroyed, and my family has been killed."

"His name is Van Helsing?" Ryan asked, the name reminding him of several of the books on his shelf. "As in the monster hunter?"

"Aye. Steven is his descendant, one of many."

"Wait, wait, back up a minute. If Van Helsing is real, then vampires, werewolves--they're all real, too?"

"I'm afraid so."

Ryan fell silent. *Real. All of them. They can't be, can they? They're just stories. I've been reading about them my entire life. It's just Boss that's real, right?*

"Do you have a name?" Boss asked.

Ryan nodded, though he was still trying to collect his thoughts. "Well yeah, just like you. Your name *is* Boss, right?"

"My kind called me Montra Bos."

"Montra Bos?"

"Aye. 'Boss' is just what I'm called by the few humans I know."

"I… I think I'll stick to Boss, too."

"If you would prefer, then fine. You?"

Ryan relaxed against his bed. "Ryan."

"Well, Ryan, despite our current situation, and your harsh words, it is good to meet you."

Boss looked around the room until his stare fell on Ryan's bookshelf. "It seems werewolves and vampires are nothing new to you."

"Yeah," Ryan replied with a shrug. "I like scary stories. My grandpa used to tell me all kinds about vengeful ghosts, werewolves, wendigo…" He smiled.

"I guess that's why I think it's all so interesting."

"Your grand--*pa*?"

"Yeah. Grandpa. You know, my parent's parent? Look." He grabbed the family photo from his bedside table, then held it in his lap and pointed at each face so Boss could see. "There's me, my mom, and my--"

"Magnus!"

Ryan stopped, his finger hovering over his grandfather's face. "Yeah? That's my grandpa."

"Of all the people I could have accidentally stuck to," Boss began with a chuckle, "It's someone related to Magnus."

"You knew him?"

"Aye! A seasoned monster hunter. He was there the day my village fell. He saved my life."

Ryan laughed, genuinely amused. "Now I know you're lying to me. He didn't hunt monsters; he hunted elk. Deer. You know, normal animals."

"He hunted much more dangerous things than mere elk, Ryan. The day I met him, he was hunting a creature near my home that was responsible for killing humans in the surrounding areas."

Ryan looked down at the picture. What Boss was saying-- It couldn't be true, could it? His grandfather was a normal man. Sure he used to leave town for days, sometimes weeks at a time, but he'd always said he was going on hunting trips.

"We must go to him," Boss continued. "He knows me and my fight with Steven. He can help us find my body, and get the amulet back."

"We can't." An all too familiar sadness returned to Ryan, tears welling in his eyes as he set the photo back onto his bedside table.

"What do you mean, we can't? He's--"

41

"He's gone."

"Gone where?"

"Gone to…" Ryan paused, his eyes burning. "He-- He had a bad heart attack last year. It killed him before he even hit the ground." Ryan rested his head against the bedside and stared at the ceiling with tears in his eyes.

"This can't be," Boss whispered.

"Trust me," Ryan replied. "I wish he was still here too, but he's not. Sorry to tell you, but we're on our own."

And with that, they said no more.

CHAPTER 3

Ryan climbed to his feet, the sound of screeching tires outside. He peered through his bedroom window. Boss, still hovering over his face, followed his gaze. A silver truck had parked in the driveway.

The tightness in Ryan's chest loosened its grip ever so slightly at the sight of the woman exiting the driver's side door. "It's my mom," he said. *She'll know how to help us!*

But as quickly as the relief came, it vanished. *She's... totally been in this situation before, right?*

He pulled away from the window. "What am I gonna tell her?"

"Nothing," Boss replied plainly.

"If you knew my grandpa, won't she know you?"

"We've never met. The less people that know about me, the better."

"But…"

"No," Boss said; the authority in his voice almost made it seem as if he might follow it up with a threat. "This needs to stay a secret."

Ryan opened his mouth to retort, but he couldn't find the words. Considering he had almost been shot and killed earlier, this seemed like something he should tell his mom. But how would he explain why he hadn't been at school? Why he was out in the woods? What would his mother say if he told her that he heard gunshots and followed the sounds with nothing but a pocket knife? Heck, that he'd followed them at all? As much as he hated to admit it, Boss was right.

He let out an aggravated sigh. "Fine, fine. It's a need-to-know basis. I got it."

Boss huffed before fading away, and just then Ryan's bedroom door opened. He turned around to see his mom peeking in with a furrowed brow. "Hey, honey."

"H-hey mom!" Ryan squeaked.

"Who you talkin' to?"

"Oh, just… you know. Thinkin' out loud."

She nodded, though she still appeared confused. "Why are you home and not at school?"

Ryan frowned, dropping his head. "I, uhh…" He paused, remembering everything Todd said to him back in class. "It wasn't a very good day. Todd was…" He stopped there, didn't need to say any more.

She offered him a reassuring expression, the kind Ryan imagined most mothers gave their children in situations like this, to let the kids know that they had someone on their side. "I'm sorry, Ry."

He forced a weak smile. "It's okay. Tomorrow's a new day, right?"

She smiled back. "Yeah, it is."

"Speaking of being home early, what are you doing here?"

She rolled her eyes. Something must be irritating her. "I came to grab some clothes and things. They have me doing another all-nighter at the hospital." She raised her fingers to her head like a gun, pretending to shoot herself.

Ryan chuckled a little. "No rest for the wicked, right?"

"Not when you're a nurse in *this* town. Especially lately. There've been some weird ones coming in. More than normal."

Ryan narrowed his eyes. The "weird ones" were patients at the hospital, either living or dead, that he had occasionally heard her mention around his grandpa when the old man had still been alive. "Weird how?"

"Oh, you know, injuries from unlikely animal attacks. Strange bites, things like that. We get some every great now and then, but lately it's been pretty consistent. Hopefully there isn't some freaky creature lurking near town. Be careful on your way to school and back, okay?"

"Yeah, sure," Ryan replied, nodding.

"Maddie is getting held overnight too, so make sure to let Chyann know in case she needs to come over for dinner. I'm gonna leave you money for pizza or Larry's."

Ryan nodded again. "Sounds good. Thanks, mom."

"I'll see you tomorrow, okay?"

"Sure. Love you."

"Love you too," she called as she closed the door, and once Ryan was sure she'd left the house, he rubbed his temples and sighed, wandering toward his desk.

Soon Boss reappeared. "The child of Magnus Myers," he whispered, almost as though he were in awe.

There was a buzzing at the desk, and they glanced over. It was Ryan's cell, with Chyann's name visible on the screen.

Boss gave the device a quizzical look as Ryan picked it up. "What is that?"

"It's my phone," Ryan said. "My friend is calling me."

"Well, ignore it. We have bigger problems to deal with right now."

"Like what? Getting unstuck?"

"*Obviously*," Boss hissed.

"Well, to track down Helsing and find your body, we're gonna need help, so I should tell my friends what's going on."

Boss's eye went wide. "Absolutely not!"

"If I can't tell my mom, then at least let me tell my friends. We can trust them, I promise." Before Boss could say another word, Ryan swiped the screen to answer the call and pressed the phone to his ear. "Hey, Chy."

"End the talk now," Boss whispered, his tone furious.

"Hey, Ry! What's up?" Chyann chirped on the other end.

"I said end it," Boss hissed again.

Ryan lowered the device and whispered back at Boss, trying to sound just as intimidating as the Ooawan. "No."

"Do it!"

"No." He put the phone back to his ear. "Just sitting at home watching TV. You?"

"Will and I are out of class for the day. We were thinking of heading your way and watching movies the rest of the night. How does that sound?"

"That sounds--" Ryan couldn't finish the sentence. His body jerked to one side, then again to the other, and he almost lost his balance. As if by some other-worldly force, because he certainly wasn't doing it, his left arm lifted itself, reaching as though to grasp the phone. Ryan resisted, holding the device up and away from his ear.

"Are *you* doing that?" he whispered irritably at Boss.

"Don't make me smash that thing," the Ooawan replied.

Ryan's left leg kicked involuntarily, as if it were trying to make him walk, and the movement nearly sent him plummeting into the floor. "Stop!" he yelled, struggling to stay standing, stumbling all around the room.

"Ry? Are you okay?" Chyann asked.

"Yeah, I'm fine," Ryan answered through clenched teeth.

"Stop talking to her," Boss ordered.

"Is there somebody over there with you?" Chyann continued.

"No! It's just the--" His left leg kicked, and he fell hard, back-first onto the carpet. He dropped his phone, the wind knocked out of him.

"The less people who know about me, the better," Boss said. "If you tell your friends and Helsing finds them, he will torture or even *kill* them if it means finding you and me. Are you willing to put them in that kind of danger?"

Ryan wheezed, trying to respond, but not enough breath would draw. His throat remained locked. He rolled over onto his stomach and managed to choke out a few measly breaths, then crawled toward his phone.

"Ry? Are you there?" Chyann asked. Ryan reached with both arms toward the phone, but Boss didn't manage to take control this time because Ryan was able to scoop up the device with his right hand. He brought it to his ear and rolled over, onto his back.

"TV… It's just the TV, sorry." His left arm clawed for the phone again, but he fought to keep it.

"Is everything okay?"

"Oh, yeah. Totally fine! What time are you guys gonna be here?" His left arm fell limp, Boss finally defeated.

"We can get there in about twenty minutes."

"Sounds great. See you then." He hung up quickly and dropped the phone. "Really?" he asked Boss through tired breaths.

"Do what you want. Tell them everything and get them killed. I don't care anymore."

Ryan balled his fists. "Those two are my best friends. We've known each other basically since we were born. Even if I told them, I know that no matter how crazy or messed up all this is, they would be there for me. That means they would be there for you, too."

Boss snorted. "I have nothing more to say to you. I've made my stance on the matter clear."

"Does your whole species have an attitude?"

"My whole species is *dead*!"

At this outburst, Ryan's stomach fell. "Wait, what?

"Helsing. He wiped out my village, remember? He and his family. Everyone I knew. Everyone I loved. Slaughtered, butchered, killed."

Ryan fell silent, the weight of Boss's words hitting him. He'd heard what the Ooawan had said earlier, but he didn't think he'd fully understood the gravity of the situation until now. *I know he said his family was killed, but I didn't realize…*

Ryan's chest tightened with guilt. Losing your family was bad enough, but your entire species? That had to be on a whole other level. "So, when you said he destroyed your village, you mean he destroyed everything? He killed your family *and* everybody else?"

"The Helsings stormed our village with guns, weapons we weren't able to fight. They burned our trees and homes with fire, and they murdered every single one of my kind they found. As far as I'm aware, I'm the only one who made it out alive, and it's all thanks to Magnus."

They sat quietly for a minute or two. *I can't even begin to imagine what that must feel like.* Although when Ryan really started to think about it, he could kind of envision it. He thought of his friends, his mother, and anyone else he had ever remotely cared for, all gone in the blink of an eye.

If what Boss says is true, he really does owe my grandpa. He pressed his lips into a thin line. *If only he was here… He would know what to do. He always knew what to do.*

"Look, I won't tell my friends anything about this tonight," Ryan said, and Boss perked up a bit. "I'm gonna have to at some point though, you know? This isn't something I can just hide from everybody. Especially if you're gonna go and move me around like that. Tonight though, I just… I need to shut off for a little while. Pretend the weirdest, craziest, scariest day of my life never happened."

Boss considered this for a bit and, despite the fact that they still seemed to be two entirely separate beings, Ryan sensed that Boss was maybe starting to agree with him.

"Aye, I think I understand. It may not seem like it, but I feel… tired. This-- Whatever this is between us is strange, and I'm not entirely sure how… I don't…" He let out a sound like a growl. "All I know right now is that I feel exhausted, that I need to rest. I'm going to try and do just that. Hopefully I can. We both deserve a night of peace after all this, aye?"

"You can say that again."

Boss knit his brow. "Why would I say it again? I said it just now."

"It's… nevermind."

"Well, I'll try to be aware of what's going on. If you need me, just call for me."

"Sure."

Boss faded away, retreating to wherever it was he went when he wasn't hovering over Ryan's face, and Ryan rested his head against the fluffy carpet and closed his eyes. "What did I get myself dragged into?"

After that, the night was much more relaxed. Chyann and Willy stopped by around fifteen minutes after Boss faded away, and the fun began almost immediately. Two comedies and one horror movie later, the terrifying series of events in the woods earlier that day seemed like no more than a bad dream.

However, throughout the night Ryan would remember. His stomach would clench, the feeling of an ice-cold gun barrel pressed against his head coming out of nowhere, and if there were any sort of clicking noises, his hair would stand on end.

It seemed like anything had the potential to take him right back to those woods. To that glade. Every so often, he would even feel Boss's presence shift in the back of his mind, as though the Ooawan had woken from a deep slumber, only to glance through Ryan's eyes to check on the commotion before returning to his sleep.

Through it all though, Chyann and Willy managed to keep Ryan's spirits high, helping him put his unease to rest even if only for a few moments before its return. Ultimately he'd faced something chilling, and he knew deep down it may not be over. There was a maniac named Steve Helsing out there that would be looking for him, and a monster whose soul had somehow bonded to him. And if what Boss said about vampires and werewolves and other supernatural creatures was true, there were even worse things out there than Helsing.

But none of that mattered now, because Ryan wasn't alone. Right now, he was with his friends.

CHAPTER 4

Bright morning sun shone through the windows of Larry's Diner. It hurt Steve's eyes, and his head. He leaned back, raising his newspaper just enough to shield his sight. *Of course I pick the seat where the sun is gonna be a pain in my ass.*

He glanced up to see his waitress walking past the booths and tables with a full pot of steaming coffee. She seemed nice enough when Steve first entered the diner and was slightly overweight, with a bright red blouse and matching skirt, not to mention a powerful lavender perfume that choked him every time she walked by. She would probably be by soon to check up on him. However, he had more pressing matters to attend to right this moment, like finding out more about this dump of a mountain town.

He scanned the headlines and articles of the paper. *Why here? Of all the places the cat could have chosen to go to, to hide in, why Twilight Peak?*

It didn't make any sense to Steve. He had been tracking Boss's travels for months, and the cat had been moving all over the place. Zigzags, straight paths, whatever he could do to shake Steve loose. None of it had worked, of course. Tracking was one of the very first things Steve had learned as a kid. Following Boss's attempts at escape was child's play.

But somewhere around two months ago, the cat seemed to have gotten desperate. He changed his direction and moved straight here. *Why? What was here that he came for?* Steve couldn't get the question out of his mind.

It appeared there may be supernatural activity across this town, almost more than in other places. Missing people, strange deaths, abandoned buildings with shady histories. You name it, Twilight Peak had it. Could that be the reason the cat chose this place?

He clicked his tongue and crumpled the paper in his fist, then tossed it back onto the table. It wasn't like the goddamn thing was helping, anyway. Science fairs, the town's history month, and a new exhibit at the local museum? Could this place seem any more *boring*?

The sun crept up, blinding him again. Pain flared behind his eyes, and now his shoulder too, thanks to that little brat from yesterday. He lifted one hand to gently massage the injury. *Probably have to clean it again here soon.* The bandages he'd stolen from a nearby gas station were cheap, and it was beginning to show. The stab wound was small, but it bled. It bled a lot. So much so that it had already leaked through these chintzy wrappings despite having been changed only an hour before he sat down at this very booth.

"More coffee, sir?" The voice of the waitress would have been a surprise since he was so deep in thought, but the tidal wave of lavender had reached him long before she did.

He offered her his sweetest smile, sliding his nearly empty mug toward her. "Please."

She nodded with a smile of her own, then poured him some. As she walked away, he stifled a gag. *Does she bathe in that crap?*

He took a drink, but stopped as his wound pulsed with hot pain. *I still can't believe I let that little maggot stab me*, he thought, lowering his mug as he continued massaging his shoulder.

The more he contemplated what had happened, the more it pissed him off. He hadn't seen the pocket knife. Wasn't even paying attention. He'd still been riding the high that came with shooting that uptight furball dead. Just like the kid, the cat had slipped through his fingers.

It was fine, though. It just meant he had to improvise. Wouldn't be the first time, and it certainly wouldn't be the last. Plus he did have a possible advantage-- He had that amulet. Whatever the cat did, there was a chance it could be reversed. All magic was like that, even magic as powerful as whatever kind of juice was in that hunk of mystical junk.

Loading the corpse into his truck had proven to be difficult with a bum shoulder, but one thing was for sure: It was the smart move. After all, it was better to be smart. Father had beaten many things into him and his siblings growing up, but being stupid was not one of them.

His cell phone buzzed on the table, and he looked over. Adamson was calling. Again. *Speaking of family...*

Steve slid the screen, ignoring the call. He wasn't sure how many times Adamson had tried to contact him now. Count had been lost a few weeks ago, and he'd ignored upwards of fifty calls from his older brother one day.

The pulsing behind his eyes and in his shoulder grew worse. *Cheap bandages, cheap painkillers. I'm definitely not going back to steal from* that *gas station again.*

He took another sip of his coffee and gazed through the window, the sunlight finally simmering down, to see three figures as they walked by. *Wait a minute... Is that...*

Steve coughed and spit out his drink, then narrowed his eyes and leaned toward the window. There was no mistaking it, even from this angle. He didn't recognize the girl, or the kid with the mohawk, but the third kid, the one in the middle... There was no doubt about it. It was the brat that stabbed him yesterday.

Steve grinned so wide he thought he probably looked like the Grinch from that old animated special. "Well break my neck..." he whispered. The kid with the mohawk didn't have anything on him, but the girl and the brat both had backpacks. *I was so caught up in my pain and losing the cat I didn't even consider the fact that the kid was gonna be a sitting duck, all thanks to the good ol' educational system.*

Steve quickly rose from his booth, took a few dollars from his wallet, and tossed them onto the table, then exited the diner, throwing on his dark hat and trench coat.

The sun, as assaulting as ever, suddenly seemed more welcoming. Here he was trying to get his head on straight, and his prey just so happened to stroll right on by his seat. No need for improv if shit just fell into his lap!

Granted, he had to stay a bit behind them so he wouldn't be spotted, but that didn't stop the pep in his step. And to think he'd had to drag himself into that diner an hour or two ago. Now he was practically skipping with excitement. Revenge was on the horizon! He just had to let these twits lead him to the school, and then he'd set up a watch.

There would be time to plan his next move while they were asking for prom dates and gossiping in the halls.

Ryan faded from the conversation, his thoughts drifting. *"I don't like this,"* Boss said, his words echoing in Ryan's mind. *"You're outside in the open, and Helsing knows what you look like."*

"I know, but I can't just hide in my house forever," Ryan said. *"I have to act like nothing is going on, right?"*

"If he finds you, he will hurt you. He'll hurt anyone who gets in his way."

"He was going to shoot me. Trust me, I get the idea." He adjusted his backpack strap over his shoulders as

he continued walking down the pavement with his friends. Coffee shops, clothing boutiques, restaurants, and apartment buildings sat high on either side of the street. It was another few minutes worth of walking before they would arrive at the front doors of Mountain's Point High School.

Twilight Peak was an old town. As far as Ryan was concerned, it had been here since the beginning of time. The brickwork and construction of almost every building demanded modern day renovation, and yet they all otherwise still stood strong without much wear or tear found. The sidewalks were red round-bricked to perfection rather than the usual flat gray cement you would expect to see, and the street lights on every corner of the roads looked like lampposts from Victorian London.

Time continued moving forward, and for some reason, Twilight Peak refused to move with it.

Willy's voice suddenly snapped Ryan back to reality. "Earth to Ry!" the boy shouted in his ear.

Ryan flicked his head up, cheeks warm as he turned toward his friend. "Sorry, I was, uhhh… somewhere else."

"You're tellin' me." Willy laughed a little. "I was talkin' to ya for like two straight minutes and you didn't say anything."

Ryan chuckled, and Chyann nudged his shoulder. "I know I've asked like a bunch of times already, but are you sure you're okay? You seem to be really… well, in your head, since last night." She wore a similar plaid shirt to the one she'd had on the day before, but now sported a light purple tank top underneath.

Ryan nodded, forcing a smile. "Yeah, I'm fine. I

just have a lot on my mind right now." Chyann gave him a look of uncertainty, but didn't press further.

As the trio ascended the stone stairs into the school, Ryan spied a building mounted taller than the trees nearby. Construction workers had been erecting it for the past few weeks. It was just a skeleton of a structure, not yet complete and void of finished windows and walls, with scaffolding that rose beside it like vines twisting up a garden fence. It didn't appear all that wide, and the only thing Ryan could really compare it to was a rectangle turned on its end. He guessed it was going to be an office building or something residential. He didn't really know, but he had heard some teachers talking in the halls recently about the distraction the noises of its construction had caused their classes.

Ryan pushed thoughts of the new place out of his mind as he and his friends passed through the main entrance. After all, he had more important things to concern himself with right now.

"William Wylee!" The trio stopped, turning back to see a woman leaning out from the main office window, next to the entrance. She gestured for Willy to make his way there. "Principal Bullworth needs to see you."

Willy turned to Ryan and Chyann with a guilty smile and shrug. "Sorry amigos, looks like the warden wants to see me in his office again."

"Don't you get sick of morning detention?" Ryan asked.

"Well, duh," Willy replied. "What I *don't* get sick of is driving all the teachers crazy when they get lucky enough to sit in a room with me every morning." The

three laughed, then fist bumped before Willy sauntered off. "Say a prayer for me." And with that the boy
disappeared into the office.

Ryan and Chyann shrugged at one another as they
turned and continued walking into the cafeteria filled
with students, teachers, and tables. A short line had
assembled from the room nearby where the food was
set out for students to buy.

"You want breakfast?" Ryan asked.

Chyann shook her head. "I don't think I'm desperate enough for whatever goop they have up there."

Ryan let out a single dry chuckle. "Wish I could
say the same."

"Just grab an extra milk for me," Chyann said, and
handed him a dollar. "I'll go save our table."

Ryan took the money and walked off to get in line.
He grabbed a tray as Chyann headed toward their
usual seats at the back of the cafeteria. Once he got
far enough in line to start snagging food, he began
gathering items and placing them on his tray, including two cartons of milk, his arms aching all the while.
Come to think of it, his whole body was still sore
from yesterday, and it had started to drive him crazy.

As he progressed up the line, a standout shooting
pain arced through his skull, and he stopped and
clamped his eyes shut. He pressed a palm against his
forehead, hoping it would help. As he stood there,
Boss's voice sounded in his thoughts once again:

"*This feeling...*"

"It hurts," Ryan replied.

"*It feels... like when I transferred my soul out of my
body, into yours.*"

Ryan managed to force his eyes open a crack and

glanced around the cafeteria, the feeling slowly fading, then moved forward in line despite the fact that the sensation hadn't completely dissipated yet.

"Perhaps the amulet is close by," Boss suggested.

"Is that why it hurts so bad all of a sudden?"

"The pain yesterday seemed to have lessened after you ran away from Helsing. Perhaps…"

Somebody bumped into Ryan from behind, and he dropped his tray. It clattered to the floor.

He swung around. "Hey! Watch where…" He trailed off, his stomach dropping when he saw who had run into him.

Todd Hallow towered over Ryan with a sneer. "What was that, creep?"

The bully stepped closer, and Ryan backed up. "C'mon, Todd. Not today."

"What were you gonna say to me, huh?" He shoved Ryan. "You feelin' tough?"

"Seriously dude, just back off, all right?"

Todd didn't listen. Instead, the bully shoved Ryan again, harder this time, and the boy slammed into a kid ahead of him in line. "Or what?" Todd asked. "What are you gonna do if I don't back off?"

Students began to look over and gather around them, including Chyann, who appeared pretty irritated as she stood from her chair and stomped toward the commotion. *Oh great, that's just what I need*, Ryan thought. *Someone else coming to save me yet again.*

Todd leaned down, so close to Ryan he could smell sour chocolate milk on the bully's breath. "You gonna beat me up, creep?"

"Defend yourself," Boss commanded.

"Are you kidding? I can't fight Todd. He's twice my size!"

60

"*Forelta Le Von,*" Boss said, irritation lacing his tone. It almost sounded as if he were cursing.

Suddenly and very involuntarily, Ryan reached up and shoved Todd. The bully stumbled backward, seemingly caught off guard, but managed to catch his balance. The crowd of students cooed in surprise; Chyann stopped nearby, watching the scene with wide eyes.

Todd's smile faded, and panic shot through Ryan's body. What he'd just done was practically a death sentence, and he hadn't even been the one who'd committed the crime.

"*Boss, why would you do that?*" he cried internally.

"*Just relax,*" Boss replied.

Todd popped his knuckles, moving closer. "You wanna go to the nurse's office? 'Cause I can arrange that."

"*He's not kidding,*" Ryan thought at Boss. "*You're worried about Steve killing us, but Todd has put me in the hospital twice before!*"

Todd positioned himself as though to push Ryan, but just before he could make contact, Ryan's arms whipped up and swatted Todd away, then raised themselves again and shoved the bully once more, harder than before.

Todd stumbled, nearly falling before catching himself. Other students started laughing, and he swung around with an angry glare, silencing the guffawing right after it began.

"*Boss, you have to stop,*" Ryan pleaded. "*I'm not strong enough to win against this guy!*"

"*So you say.*"

Todd turned toward Ryan with white-knuckled

fists. "You have no idea what you're getting into right now."

The bully leapt forward, throwing a high punch, and yellow flashed in Ryan's peripheral, whatever little control he'd had over his body gone now. Without thinking, without trying, Ryan ducked beneath Todd's massive swing. He balled his hands and punched Todd once, twice in the gut, then hopped backward, out of the bully's reach.

Todd groaned and kneeled over. Their peers began laughing once again, and some even cheered. Ryan glanced at Chyann. She smiled as if mildly surprised.

"Okay..." Ryan thought at Boss. *"That was kinda cool."*

"It's a simple move, really."

Todd gained his composure and steadied himself, stroking his stomach a few times before shooting Ryan a loathsome glare. "Okay, creep. Forget the nurse. You're going straight to the freaking graveyard!" He rushed forward, hurling another high punch.

However, Boss took control yet again. The Ooawan made Ryan maneuver under and out of harm's way, and for a moment Ryan wondered if perhaps he was dreaming. The feeling of his body moving not of his own accord felt so fantastical and otherworldly, it was hard to believe any of this could really be happening.

Todd swung once more, but rather than ducking, Boss made Ryan step back this time. Boss shifted under the swing and kicked out Todd's knee. The bully fell. Yellow flashed in Ryan's peripheral once more. As Todd looked up, Ryan--or rather, Boss--delivered a single punch to the bully's jaw. The blow sent Todd to the floor, blood flying from his lips.

The yellow glow in his vision began to fade. At the same time, his limbs grew noticeably heavier, and after curling some fingers he realized it must be because Boss was relinquishing control of his body.

The cafeteria erupted into cheers, laughter, a few boos, and more. Ryan swung around to look at everyone. He spied Chyann at the back of the throng, clapping excitedly, and the corners of his mouth turned up in a smile. Was this how performers on TV felt on a daily basis? For once some of his peers were praising him; for once he wasn't the freak of the school. It felt... good.

"Physical prowess isn't everything," Boss said. *"Muscle doesn't always determine the victor of a fight."*

"I'm a believer," Ryan replied as he scanned the horde. However, his satisfaction didn't last. The principal and a few teachers were making their way toward him and Todd, pushing through the crowd of students.

"Oh, crap." He swerved around and rushed down the hall right of the cafeteria. How could he be so stupid? Of course Bullworth was going to come around. Had he really forgotten teachers existed? He may have slipped away for now, but it was only a matter of time before Todd told them Ryan had been involved in the cafeteria fight.

He panted, flying past classrooms and lockers. *Now I'm gonna be right next to Willy on the top of Bullworth's list. Between the principal, Todd, and Steve, I'm practically a dead man walking.*

Finally he reached the exit leading out to the football and track field. After everything that had just occurred, a little fresh air was just what he needed.

Chyann could hardly believe what she'd just witnessed, yet the proof was right before her. Hopefully the principal and teachers hadn't seen Ryan among the crowd as he made his escape. *That's the last thing he needs*, she thought. *Suspension for standing up for himself.*

Principal Bullworth was a large man, but not in the sense of weight so much as height, and he towered above most of the students as he arrived at Todd's side to help the boy to his feet. Chyann turned instinctively, unsurprisingly finding Willy as he approached her.

"Whooooaa," Willy said. "It's about damn time somebody gave it to Todd. Who's the champ that knocked him offa his high horse?"

He was never going to believe who. Chyann certainly didn't. "It was Ryan," she said, practically bouncing with excitement.

Willy chuckled and tapped her shoulder. "Yeah, sure. Seriously though Chy, who was it?"

She gave him the most serious look she could muster and waited for him to catch up. His mouth formed an "o" and she figured he must have finally realized she wasn't kidding. "No freakin' way."

Chyann nodded. If she hadn't seen the fight herself, she would have reacted the same. For as long as she'd known Ryan, he'd never stood up against Todd's abuse. The rare times he did had led to disaster, and most of the time it came down to Chyann having to stop Todd from pummeling Ryan into a bloody pulp.

She didn't mind of course, as Ryan was practically her brother, and she'd be damned if anyone was going to treat her brother like a punching bag.

However, something about this situation felt… off. The way Ryan had moved around Todd was so graceful it was as if he'd been in hundreds of fights, and that was far from the Ryan she knew. He didn't have the brawler style that Willy did, and he certainly didn't have the self defense training that she did.

He's been acting really strange since last night, too, she thought. *Something isn't right.*

She grabbed Willy's arm to pry his attention away from the sight of Bullworth hauling Todd toward the office. As nice a sight as it was, they had somewhere else they needed to be. "Come on, Will. Let's go find Ryan."

"Hell yeah," Willy said. "I gotta give him a huge pat on the back and buy him a beer."

Chyann rolled her eyes and dragged Willy away from the commotion, toward the back hall Ryan had fled through. "We're not old enough to buy a beer, let alone drink one."

Willy sighed. "C'mon, Chy. Dig deep. Find a little adventure in your tired, square-shaped soul, huh?"

Ryan slammed his shoulder against the metal doors, pushing them open before rushing out into the warm morning. When he reached the empty lot behind the school, he paused to catch his breath, and soon Boss appeared before him.

"Thanks a lot for that back there," Ryan yelled. "Now Todd's gonna be out for blood."

"Todd is the least of our worries right now," Boss countered. "Besides, I thought you were impressed?"

Ryan ran a shaking hand through his hair. It had felt amazing to take Todd down like that, even if he hadn't been completely in control, but now reality was setting in. "I said it was kinda cool, but I'm probably gonna get suspended from school because of it, and to make matters worse, Todd is gonna be hunting *me* the way Steve is hunting *you*."

The Ooawan rolled his eye. "Oh, please. I did you a favor. You were standing idle, ready to allow that young man to hurt you. It's a wonder you didn't wait around for Helsing to reload his gun back in the woods, considering how passive you are."

"Yeah? Well, I didn't ask you to do me any favors, all right?"

"Fine. Next time, I'll just let him hit you."

"Fine."

"*Fine.*" Boss faded away so abruptly it reminded Ryan of a child slamming a bedroom door during a tantrum. Not that Ryan didn't feel like throwing a fit of his own, anyway. He snarled, kicking aside a crumpled soda can.

Just as he was about to stomp away, he heard doors open behind, his chest tightening. *Great, what is it now?* he thought, and turned around. However, once he saw who'd followed him outside, at least half of his anger subsided.

Chyann and Willy hurried toward him, the teens

grinning ear to ear. "That was amazing," Chyann exclaimed, then threw her arms around his neck. "But where in the world did you learn how to fight?"

Ryan hugged her back. "I dunno. It just kinda, uh… It just kinda happened." She pulled away and raised a brow in suspicion, but he simply shrugged. Sure, he wasn't telling her everything, but he wasn't exactly lying either.

"I know what's goin' on here," Willy said.

Ryan's heart skipped, afraid his friend had already discovered his secret. He and Chyann turned toward Willy. "You do?" they asked in unison.

The boy with the mohawk sauntered toward Ryan, a mischievous expression on his face. "Yeah, I do. You…" He paused for dramatic effect, and Ryan held his breath. "… were bit by a radioactive bug, and now you've got super powers!"

Ryan laughed and relaxed his shoulders, though some jitters remained. "Funny, Will," he said. "Very funny."

"Oh, come on, bro," Willy continued, "Think about it. The hero always beats down his bully just before he dons a mask and starts wiping crime off the streets."

"Do you hear yourself right now?" Chyann asked.

Willy flexed a bicep. "I could be your handsome sidekick. And Chy can be… uhhh… Chy."

"He's not a superhero," Chyann said with finality.

"Yeah, as far as you know," Willy argued.

Chyann raised a hand as if to signal the boy to stop being so silly, then faced Ryan, her expression serious. "C'mon, Ry. What's up?"

Ryan fidgeted, unsure of how to answer. If there was a time to tell them what was really going on, this was it… right?

"Yeah, Ry," the familiar voice of a man called to them from nearby. The sound sent chills down Ryan's spine. *It can't be.*

The trio turned toward the voice. Steve Helsing, complete with his dark hat and trench coat, leaned against the closest school building wall. Ryan's jaw dropped, his breath catching in his throat.

Steve strolled toward them, smiling devilishly. "What's up, brat? The cat got your tongue?" Chyann and Willy creased their brows, sharing a confused look, while Steve lowered his head and smirked at Ryan from under the brim of his hat. "Did our mutual friend beat up your little school bully?"

Ryan swallowed hard. "How did you find me?"

Steve spread out his arms. "Are you serious? You're walkin' around in broad daylight"--he circled the trio, pointing at his own face--"and I know what you look like. I made a nice mental picture of ya right before you stabbed me."

Chyann and Willy stared at Ryan in bewilderment, their expressions practically begging for an explanation, but he couldn't provide one right now. His mind raced almost as fast as his heart, and the standout shooting pain in his skull had returned, throbbing worse than ever. He was starting to have trouble focusing.

Steve stopped his wandering to face Ryan head-on. "You had to have known I was looking for you, right? I mean, I'm not exactly gonna go home empty handed just because you got your peanut butter all mashed up with the cat's jelly, y'know?"

Ryan seized Chyann's and Willy's wrists and started backing away. Willy leaned over to Chyann. "See, I told you Ry was a superhero," he whispered. "He's already got an arch nemesis." Chyann slapped the boy on the arm.

Steve stepped closer. "Oh, don't worry. I don't have beef with either of you." He reached into his trench coat and pulled out Boss's amulet, then held it high above his head. "**Ipsum Revelare!**" The amulet flashed bright red, and Boss materialized over Ryan's face. At the sight of the Ooawan, Chyann and Willy yelped and stumbled backward.

Steve grinned, lowering the amulet as he locked his gaze onto Boss. "But I do have beef with him."

CHAPTER 5

Chyann and Willy stared in shock at the ghostly Ooawan's face shadowed over Ryan's, then shared an unsure look with one other, clearly trying to make sense of the scene unfolding before them. Ryan wanted to explain, to tell them everything. But right now wasn't a good time.

Steve, who stood nearby, wrapped the talisman's chain around his hand and gave Boss a smug smile. His dark hat cast sinister shadows over his face. "You thought you were clever jumping ship, didn't ya?" Boss snorted, and Steve continued, "Unfortunately for you, I found your little trinket, and a spell that just might reverse its effects."

"I'm surprised a simple mind like yours can even

understand such complex magic," Boss said, his tone surprisingly calm considering their current predicament.

At this comment, Steve cackled, while Chyann and Willy shared another surprised look. Ryan figured the appearance of Boss alone had probably sent them reeling, but hearing the Ooawan not only speak, but speak so well, was most likely driving them even farther down the path of bewilderment.

"Took the words right outta my mouth, bud," Steve yelled, laughing, then motioned to Ryan. "So how about it, kid? You want him out, right?" The man held the amulet up and jangled it loudly. "I found out how to do it. Here's your chance."

Ryan gulped, unsure of what course of action to take next. *He found out how to do it? Does he seriously mean he can split Boss and I back up?*

Steve lowered the talisman to admire it. "I had plenty of time to research this old thing while I waited for you three. I gotta say, for a piece of junk, it's capable of some serious mojo. But like all serious mojo"--his stare drifted back to Boss--"it can be reversed, so long as you have the right words."

After a few moments of silence, Boss sighed, and everyone turned to him. "Listen to Helsing, Ryan. It's for the best. This is my fight, not yours. We clearly can't continue this way."

Ryan lowered his head. Boss was giving up. The boy could tell this was sincere. He sensed what Boss was feeling-- Guilt, but also peace. He was willing to give himself up without a fight.

"Listen to him, kid," Steve said. "Come quietly, let me do my thing, and I'll let you walk away. No harm, no foul. Which is pretty kind for me since, you know." He tapped his shoulder. "That *really* hurt."

But Ryan only stood there, saying nothing. What should he do? What was right? And how could the Ooawan just give up to Steve like this? *If Boss is telling the truth, then this guy destroyed everything he knew. Steve has killed hundreds, and Boss is just going to go along without a fight?*

Ryan bit his lip. *If grandpa Magnus were here, what would he do?*

Willy stepped between Ryan and Steve. "Does somebody wanna tell us what's goin' on exactly?"

"Your friend can explain later," Steve replied, chuckling. "Right now we gotta take care of something."

"If I come with you," Boss began, "You have to promise to let Ryan and the others go without harm."

"Didn't I already say I would?" Steve asked in mock confusion.

"We both know you aren't a man of your word," Boss snapped back with a sharp glare.

The corner of Steve's mouth turned up into a grin. "Is that what you've been tellin' these kids about me? That I'm just some evil, lying, crazy man?"

"You were going to shoot a child," Boss yelled.

Chyann and Willy went wide eyed, but Steve just shrugged the accusation off. "I jumped the gun. Look kid, I'm sorry I tried to shoot you in the head, okay? I didn't know then what I know now. So come on. Let's do this, huh?" Ryan stared down at the concrete for a moment, then slowly looked up, his eyes meeting Steve's. The man beckoned Ryan with his free hand.

The answer was clear, the choice obvious. Ryan knew what he had to do. "No."

Steve smiled, tilting his head to one side. "I'm sorry, I must have misheard you. What was that?"

"You heard me just fine," Ryan said, with more confidence coursing through his system than ever before. He wasn't going to let this man hurt Boss, consequences be damned.

"Come on kid, you don't *really* want the cat swimming around in your head forever, do you?"

Ryan clenched his fists. "No I don't, but I'm not gonna hand him over to you either." Steve's smile finally began to fade.

"Ryan, this is our best option," Boss argued. "You have to let me go."

"No," Ryan replied. "We'll find another way."

Steve's mouth twitched until he'd forced his smile back into place, then playfully pointed a finger at Ryan. "I get it. You're still mad that I tried to shoot you. You're not ready to forgive me." He raised his hands. "Hey, that's okay. I totally understand. I'm a bit of a 'shoot first, ask questions later' kinda guy. Obviously." Slowly, he took a few steps toward Ryan. "But there's something you should know about ol' Boss. He's on the run. He's manipulative, evil, violent, and he'll do or say whatever he can to wiggle free and run away. You might think he's the good guy here because he probably told you some stupid stories about me, but you have to know that he's doing all he can to get you on his side, just to make my life a living hell. All right?"

Ryan didn't respond, refusing to back down. However, even with all the evidence stacked against Steve, the man's words were finding ways to slip past Ryan's defenses. What if this guy was telling the truth? Ryan still didn't really know that much about Boss, not for sure.

Boss glared at Steve, but Chyann and Willy looked to Ryan, as though waiting for his response.

"How about we just make this easier on all of us," Steve started, "And take care of the cat right here, right now? Together? Besides, I'm kind of on an assignment to bring him home, and if I don't, I'll get in big trouble. It's a whole thing with a ton of drama that I don't need, you get me? So, whattaya say, kid? Let's finish this so we can all go home happy, huh?"

Ryan didn't bother forming a counterpoint. He didn't need to. All feelings considered, he'd already made up his mind. He shifted his stance, standing straight and strong, then puffed his chest as he finalized his answer. "No. He's staying with me."

Steve's grin faded again, his right cheek twitching. "Kid, look. I--"

"You heard him, dude," Willy blurted, stepping shoulder to shoulder with Ryan. "The ghost--cat-- thing, stays with us."

Ryan sensed confusion emanating from Boss, and Ryan hoped the Ooawan could feel the pride he emitted. Chyann stepped up, next to Ryan, all three together against Steve. "I don't know who you are," she began, "Who the cat-thing is, or what's even going on here, but if Ryan says no on this, then you have your answer. He stays with us."

Ryan couldn't help but smile. Chyann and Willy hadn't the slightest clue what was going on, and despite it all, they still stood with him. They trusted his judgement. He suspected they would, but knowing for sure that they were there to back him up filled him with courage all the same. This wasn't like the day before, when he'd wandered into the woods by himself. He wasn't alone now.

A sneer spread across Steve's face. It was clear he was furious, just trying to hide it, but to Ryan's surprise, the man's expression vanished almost as quickly as it had formed. Another easygoing smile replaced it, but this one was different. Ryan couldn't quite put his finger on why, but it sent a shiver down his spine.

A series of forced chortles sounded from the back of Steve's throat. "Fine. That's just fine. You know why? 'Cause I don't need your permission." He raised the amulet. "I can just make the cat go back to his body. **Exitum tuum et ad formam, unde factum est.**"

As Steve chanted, Boss cried out, his form shriveling, and Ryan yelled as well. He fell to his knees, intense pain coming over him. It felt as if his very bones had been set ablaze. Steve continued spouting in that unknown language, and Ryan's pain grew worse, his vision fading between red and black.

"Ryan, what's wrong?" he heard Chyann shout, and he tried to look up at her, but everything was a blur. All except the glowing scarlet silhouette of Steve Helsing still standing before him.

"**Ne animum tuum relinquam, inanis fiat fiet corpus tuum!**" Finally Ryan's vision began to clear, just in time to see Willy as the boy charged toward Steve. "**Et vas tuum bono domu**-- Hey!"

Willy tackled the man. They tumbled to the ground. Ryan's pain vanished, except for the familiar throbbing in his head. He gasped for breath, though it was difficult because of the tightness in his chest, and Boss disappeared entirely, the Ooawan's exhaustion apparent. Ryan felt it too. Whatever Steve had just tried on them must have sapped their strength.

All the while, Willy and Steve struggled against one another. Willy punched the man hard in the jaw. "You mess with my friends, you mess with me, jack-ass!" Steve tried to shove Willy off, but the wryly teen held firm.

"Get offa me, you little runt!" Steve yelled. He caught Willy's arm, then sent a blow into the boy's side. Willy recoiled, and Steve threw him off, onto the pavement, then leapt to his feet. Willy tried to do the same, but Steve kicked him back down, then booted him in the stomach as he tried to stand again.

Chyann grabbed Ryan from under the arms and pulled him up. Just as he gained his footing, Steve reached into his jacket and pulled out his silver colt revolver and pointed it straight for them. He placed a sole on Willy's head, keeping the boy on the ground.

"You think you're being brave, kid?" Steve asked. "'Cause you're not. What you are being is an *idiot*. It doesn't matter what you do, or what you say. I will rip that miserable monster out of you, and you know what? Just because you had to make things so difficult, I don't think I'm gonna let you walk away. Maybe I'll break your legs and let you crawl home. That is, if you're lucky."

Willy struggled under Steve's boot, but the man pressed down, his shoe making a leathery squeak. Ryan winced at the sound.

"Now," Steve continued, "Let's take this somewhere a little more private, huh? Quickly, too." He pulled the hammer back on his colt, sights trained on Ryan and Chyann. "I promise you it's loaded this time." He motioned toward a nearby gate leading away from school grounds. A tall building, the one still under construction, was visible over the nearby trees. "Move it."

Against Ryan's better judgement, he and Chyann headed that way. Steve lifted his sole from Willy's head, yanked the boy to his feet, and wrapped one arm around his neck. The man pressed his gun against Willy's temple, walking with him behind Ryan and Chyann.

They trekked through the gate and off school property, then plodded over some grass and into a short alleyway. Steve gestured at the alley, filled with shade from the vegetation overhead. "That way, go. Stop at the construction site, and keep it down. Wouldn't want me to put a bullet in your friend here, would we?" Ryan and Chyann marched through the alley toward the construction site, sharing grim looks as they traveled.

We're in big trouble now, aren't we? Ryan thought. *We can't run while Steve has his colt on Willy.* He held his breath. All they could do now was trudge on, probably to their deaths. Desperate for help, he called out to Boss in his mind: *"What do we do now?"*

"We die," Boss said.

"No, I'm serious."

"So am I. Helsing is more of a combatant than your bully, and he has a gun held to us."

"So what? We just do nothing and let him kill all of us?"

"Helsing was never going to let any of you go to begin with."

Ryan sighed. *"Well, great. You're a big help…"*

Soon they arrived at a gate connected to the surrounding fence of the construction yard. A rust-covered chain hung around the gate and the fence, holding it shut.

"Go on," Steve said, and Ryan shoved the gate in. It opened just enough for them to walk through. Chyann led the way, Ryan following close. Steve shoved Willy through and entered behind the trio, his gun trained on them the entire time.

Ryan looked up at the tall building. It stood roughly five floors high, the entryway doors just several feet ahead. He and Chyann shared another glance, then turned back to Steve.

The man was still for a few moments, saying nothing, before finally he punched Willy in the face.

Ryan's stomach clenched, panic skyrocketing through his body as his friend fell into the dirt. But before he or Chyann could react, Steve clocked him in the skull with the hard white handle of the colt.

The world blurred around Ryan. He connected with the ground, a quiet darkness overcoming him as his heavy eyelids closed.

Steve couldn't believe these kids. The brat with the cat was practically a shrivelling mess yesterday, and now he suddenly had a spine? Not to mention that short one with the mohawk had dealt quite the damaging blow to Steve's jaw. Now both were down for the count.

He turned to the girl to see her kick high and fast.

Honestly, it caught him off guard how quick she was. He raised his hands in defense, about the only thing he could do.

The force of her blow knocked the colt out of his hand. She entered a fighting stance, and not some bullshit 'I saw this in a movie once' kind of pose. Steve couldn't help but be impressed. This girl had training. She might be somewhat of a challenge. "Not bad, kid," he said.

She jumped, spinning into the air with another kick. A simple step back put him just out of her range, though. She moved in for a punch as soon as she landed. Steve blocked it with ease.

He hit her behind the knee. She went down. He kneeled and wrapped his arms around her neck, then squeezed. *Maybe I was wrong about her being a challenge after all*, he thought as she struggled in his grip. "However, it doesn't hold a candle to the stuff I was taught," he whispered smugly in her ear.

She continued flailing. He could feel her desperation, the struggle to free herself, but any effort she mustered was easily snuffed by tightening his grasp. Soon she fell limp, and Steve dropped her unconscious body to the ground. He wouldn't kill her. Not yet.

"Kids..." He leaned down and grabbed the girl under the armpits. Once he got a decent hold of her, he dragged her toward the building. Luckily, the door wasn't locked. It didn't even have a doorknob, which made it much easier for Steve to come and go. He'd picked his location well.

He glanced upward at his truck parked nearby, hidden behind some foliage just off the road closest to the building, then hauled the girl into the first room and lay her down in the center of the large open area. After finishing with her, he returned to the yard twice more to pull the other two in as well.

With all three kids in the hideout, it was time to return to his truck. *Aside from getting punched in the face and hosting two extra guests, everything's going as smooth as ever.* It wasn't often he got so lucky.

Boss escaping the first time, back at the crater that used to be the cat's village, wasn't part of the original plan. But Steve had made that work. Besides, it scored him time away from home, time to be on his own. It was a high he could never come down from.

In his glee, he couldn't help but whistle a tune reminiscent of "Bad Boyfriend" by Marsha Sparks as he walked out toward his truck. He wasn't much for music, but what could he say? Marsha had made some catchy songs. Since he left home two years ago, it was all he ever seemed to hear. She was on every single goddamn radio station. He hated it at first, but after a while the music started growing on him.

He opened the back door of his truck and collected some rope out from under the seat, then continued whistling as he shut the door, spun on his heels, and shuffled to the rear of the cargo bed. Once he got the tailgate ajar, he grabbed the body wrapped in a white sheet which lay lifeless in the bed and started pulling it out. As he did so, a hand covered in brown fur fell from the linen.

He heaved the cat's body over his shoulder, then slammed the tailgate shut and journeyed back toward the building. It was time to get to work.

CHAPTER 6

Ryan slowly opened his eyes, trying to recall the events that had just transpired.

He lay on a cold stone floor in a bare room, the only light that of faint rays streaking in from outside. His whole body throbbed with pain, but the worst of it was in his head. He raised it off the ground and glanced around, his vision spinning, then gasped at what had been sprawled beside him.

Boss's corpse.

Ryan scrambled away from the dead body as memories flooded back. *Steve really did take Boss's remains with him yesterday*, he thought, plugging his nose. The sight of the corpse alone was enough to threaten vomiting, not to mention the putrid stench now assaulting his nostrils.

Chyann and Willy sat nearby, tied back-to-back against a stone support beam, but before Ryan could climb to his feet and go to them there was a click. He turned to see Steve standing at a nearby table, the man's gun aimed for Ryan. "Don't even think about it, tough guy."

Ryan raised his hands in surrender. "Listen Steve, if you let my friends go I'll do whatever you want. All right?"

Steve gave him a strained expression coupled with a hearty shrug. "Sorry, kid. That offer is no longer on the table." The man kept his gun pointed at Ryan and finished sorting some ingredients with his free hand, then tossed them into a small metal bowl and swished it around. "Turns out I can't eject the cat without a vessel for him to enter. Not if I want him to stick around, anyway."

He walked toward Boss's corpse with the bowl in hand. Once he reached the body, he carefully poured his mixture into its bullet hole. "I thought about killing you while I could. I really did. But then I had a thought…" He put a finger to his chin. "Why let the cat go when I could just stuff him back into his body and torture him for a while? I got a second chance to put him down. Maybe I should take my time, you know? Have a little fun."

Ryan scowled. "You're sick."

"And you're annoying," the man said with a sneer. "Like, really annoying. Do I hate you specifically, or is it just kids in general?" He seemed to mull that over for a moment before continuing, "Let's get started, huh?"

Steve pulled the amulet from his coat pocket. Ryan looked to Willy and Chyann, the pair groaning as they awakened, and spotted a hammer close to Chyann's foot.

As Ryan took a moment to gather his thoughts and try to formulate a plan of action, he examined his surroundings. Aside from some walls made of wood, most of the structure appeared to be concrete and metal. It was as empty as the word could describe, besides the odd piece of equipment here and there that made the room seem bigger than it really was.

Other than the four of them, the table Steve was working out his ingredients on, and a few spare tools, the only other thing Ryan could spy from his position was a stairwell in the far back of the area.

He took another glimpse of Steve and, once he decided the coast was clear, climbed to his feet. However, Steve trained the gun on him once again. "Slow your roll, cowboy."

"If you kill me, you kill Boss," Ryan blurted. "That's not what you want, is it?"

"Huh. You know, you make a good point. If only I had some third factor here to give me leverage or something…" He aimed the colt for Chyann and Willy. "Oh wait, that's right. I do have that. Now sit." Ryan tentatively kneeled, and Steve sighed. "We could have been a team here, kid. It would have been something great. And you just went and threw it all away for some *thing* that you clearly know nothing whatsoever about."

"I know he was telling me the truth about you," Ryan countered.

Steve snorted. "Oh, yeah? Did he mention my brother?"

"Your brother?"

"Yeah, my brother. The one that he *killed*."

Ryan shook his head. "No, no. That's wrong. He said his kind were peaceful."

Steve howled with laughter, while Chyann and Willy fully awoke and seemed to tune in to the unfolding conversation. "I can promise you he wasn't being peaceful when he drove his dagger into my sleeping brother's back. Like I told you kid, he's using you. He doesn't care about you or your friends. The only thing he cares about is saving his own hide." The man motioned at Boss's corpse and Ryan hung his head, trying to take in these words. "Well, saving his... whatever he has burrowed in your melon, anyway."

As Steve went back to gathering more ingredients on the table, Ryan glanced over at his friends. The pair pried at their ropes but couldn't get free. However, Chyann seemed to notice the hammer close by. She locked eyes with Ryan, then motioned at the tool with a tilt of her head, and Ryan waited for Steve to look away before giving her a nod.

"I know you're probably not gonna believe anything I say," Steve said, raising the talisman. "But it doesn't hurt to try. **Exitum tuum et ad formam, unde factum est**." The amulet began to glow, and with it a familiar and excruciating burning sensation had Ryan doubled over and crying out. Steve grinned with twisted glee and continued to chant.

"Stop it!" Chyann shouted, struggling against her ropes.

Willy flailed in the bindings. "Knock it off, you douchebag!"

Ryan rolled onto his side, unable to see his friends now, unable to see at all with his vision blurred so much. It was as if this feeling was taking over his senses and making it difficult to focus on anything else. It burned, throbbed, felt like he was being incinerated and steamrolled all at the same time. He yelled, over and over. His voice broke, his throat ripped raw.

Despite all this pain, Ryan sensed Boss as the Ooawan made his presence known in the boy's mind. *"Ryan... Thank you for trying to help me. I suppose this is where we part ways."*

"No!" Ryan wailed.

"There's nothing more that can be done," Boss said with gentle finality, his presence slipping away. *"I've been running for so long... I'm tired of it. I sincerely hope he lets you and your friends go."*

"Boss!"

"Goodbye Ryan, grandson of Magnus."

The Ooawan faded from Ryan's thoughts. As his soul was pulled away, a blinding white light beamed behind the boy's eyes. It filled his head, whizzed through his body, consumed him--though indescribable, he could feel it had--and he worried that soon all he would know was white light and pain.

Through it all though, Ryan forced his eyes open and raised a hand, shocked at what he saw next. Liquid white light leaked from his skin and pooled through the air like the sludge from a lava lamp before it floated forward at a leisurely pace, heading straight for Boss's corpse and Steve as the man held up the amulet.

Boss's soul, Ryan thought. *The white stuff has to be Boss's soul... I can't let Steve get it.* He grunted and rolled onto his stomach. It was a futile attempt to keep the spirit inside, but as he did so, he remembered the hammer near his friends. He looked over and spied it. *My only chance.*

Steve stood closer now, the talisman directly above Ryan as the man stepped forward. Chyann kicked the tool hard. It slid across the floor toward them. Ryan scooped it up.

"**Um essentia iterum!**"

Despite the pain still racking Ryan's body, he managed to turn, to rise to his knees and, as Steve focused on the dead body, he swung with a mad yell.

"**Daubus fit u--**"

The hammer collided with Steve's hand and knocked the amulet from his grip. The man bellowed, the object flying across the room before crashing to the floor at the edge of the unfinished stairwell. All the while, Steve cradled his fist.

In an instant, the liquid light sucked itself back into Ryan's chest and the glow faded. Relief came right away, the overbearing pain vanishing once Steve lost hold of the talisman. The dull throb that seemed to come with being so close to it remained, but at least that was manageable.

Ryan took a few shaky breaths and stumbled to his feet. Steve faced him, gun ready, but he swung the hammer once more. The blow struck the man in the elbow. He dropped the colt with a yell, and Ryan readied himself to attack again. Steve sidestepped the boy and punched him in the cheek.

Ryan tumbled back-first onto the concrete floor as Steve screamed through gritted teeth. He paced back and forth, arms pressed against his chest. "You stupid little son of a bitch!"

Ryan tightened his grip on the hammer. He reared

back the tool and pitched it straight for Steve. It slammed into the man's knee and he crumpled to the floor. Breath caught in his throat, Ryan scrambled to his feet and sprinted for the stairs. Once he reached them, he seized the amulet.

With new resolve, the boy looked over his shoulder, but any good feeling he may have accumulated from this victory dissipated at what he saw next. Steve had reequipped himself with the gun. The man was taking aim.

Ryan bounded up the stairwell, the unfinished wooden steps creaking under his weight as he ascended them.

An ear-splitting *crack* filled the air, and the wall to Ryan's right exploded in a shower of debris. But he couldn't let that stop him. He had to get away, had to keep the amulet from Steve.

As he reached the next floor, Steve's hate-filled screams echoed not far below, the sound of boots thumping growing closer and closer.

Willy finally managed to free his hand enough to reach into his jean pocket. He wrapped his fingers around the handle of his trusty Swiss army knife, relief flooding his system. *Thank God that maniac didn't frisk us.* He flicked the blade out and began working it into the ropes holding him and Chyann.

"Hurry up," Chyann whispered.

"I'm workin' on it. Keep yer freakin' panties on."

Soon the first cord snapped, freeing them. Chyann slipped out of the bindings quickly and helped Willy to stand. Once he'd gained his balance he straightened himself and brandished the pocket knife. "All right, let's go get this jackass."

Chyann put a hand on his weapon-wielding arm. "Wait, hold on. We can't leave the cat's… the thing's… body, er, here."

Her expression was stern, but Willy couldn't help protesting. "Are you serious?"

"Yes. If I caught everything they said, we need the body in order to perform the ritual that will get that thing out of Ryan"--she motioned toward the stairs--"and Ryan has the amulet, which we also need so we can do it." She walked toward the room's entrance and grabbed a loose piece of rebar pipe off the floor. "So, here's the plan. You get the body and hide it somewhere while I help Ryan."

Willy stood in disbelief. He didn't understand all that had just happened, but he did know one thing: She was right. That's how this went all the time, and he hated it.

Chyann hurried off toward the stairs, pipe in hand, and he shook his head and looked down at the corpse of the cat creature. He stuffed the Swiss army knife back into his pants. She was going off to stop a crazy guy with a gun, and he was stuck with the job of hiding a monster's dead body. He sighed. "God dammit…"

Ryan rushed up more creaky wooden stairs, toward the top floor, Steve scarily close behind him despite the man's injuries.

The boy was certain there were about five levels in this building, and he had already guessed that his climb had taken him up at least three. *I just need to get this amulet away from Steve. I need to get to the top, and then... what?* He struggled to form an answer. Aside from the pain in his head, the only other thing he felt right now was sheer panic.

As the boy hopped step after step, blood pounding in his ears, the faintest traces of Boss's presence returned in the back of his mind. *"Why?"* the Ooawan asked. *"Why risk your life for me?"*

"Because," Ryan began, *"If I'm not allowed to let Todd bully me, then you're not allowed to let Steve bully you."*

"You hardly know me. You don't even trust me."

Ryan glanced over his shoulder, back down the long unfinished flights as he continued running higher and higher. *"Yeah, well. I at least kinda like you, and I know that guy's crazy."*

Boss's presence faded, leaving Ryan alone as he reached the top floor. He stopped to scan the large empty room; in the center, a row of cement pillars supported the roof. He hurried toward them and slid behind one. Hopefully this hiding spot would buy him enough time until he could make his next move.

He held the chain of the amulet tightly and wrapped it around his fingers to keep its clanking and chiming from giving him away. As he did so, intense pain throbbed behind his eyes. Being close to the artifact was hard enough, but holding it granted him unignorable sensations.

Moments passed, and soon Ryan heard Steve as the man stumbled into the room. A clicking sound followed, and the boy held his breath. He knew all too well that noise meant the colt's hammer had been pulled back.

Steve's labored gasps echoed through the near-empty level, bouncing off each wall and support beam, and Ryan listened intently as the man dragged his boots across the wood.

There was a pause. *Steve must be standing still somewhere.* Ryan peeked around the pillar.

The man was hunched over, close to the farthest wall. He leaned against it so as to not aggravate his injured knee, one hand buried in his coat while the other had his gun ready. He swiveled his head from side to side in search, muttering curses under his breath.

Suddenly the man turned toward Ryan, and the boy jolted back behind the pillar. His heart practically stopped in his chest as he pressed himself against the beam. *Did he see me?*

The sound of limping footsteps neared Ryan's position. *He's found me. It's all over. I'm out of options...*

He looked around frantically and noticed another doorway just twenty feet ahead. Golden sunlight shone out from the room it led into, making his eyes water. *Maybe not yet.*

The boy sucked in a sharp breath and focused, suppressing his fear as best he could. There wasn't time to second-guess, to worry. He had to do this now.

Ryan bolted for the doorway. As he did so, the wall to his right spit out a chunk of debris, the gunfire so agonizingly loud his ears rang. For a brief moment he wondered if it would be better for him to just drop to the floor, to cover his head and admit defeat. He was screwed anyway, right?

No, he thought. *Surrendering is not an option. Not anymore.* Steve fired again, and the shot grazed the air next to Ryan's ear as he sprinted through the door.

As he entered the room he paused. His stomach fell to his feet, any hope or bravery he may have mustered gone in an instant. The walls here were entirely unfinished and led to a sharp drop like that of a rocky cliff poised high in the mountains. Frail yellow tape served as a guard rail of sorts, fluttering in the breeze.

Shit, he thought. *Dead end.*

He swung around to see Steve Helsing stumble into the room, colt held high. Though clearly tired now, the man grinned with twisted glee. "'Nowhere to go but up' they say."

The wind whistled all around, whispering through every unfinished crack, and Ryan glanced over the ledge momentarily, confirming a sharp drop to the ground. Parked construction vehicles sat far below, and he wondered if, when the workers finally showed up, they'd find any trace of his and his friends' murders. The thought made him sputter out a frightened breath, and he turned back to Steve.

The man aimed his colt at Ryan. "Okay, kid. Hand it over."

His grip on the chain tightened. *I can't give him the amulet. I can't give him Boss.*

"Give it to me," Steve said, his smile twitching until it disappeared completely. "*Now!*" His shout seemed to shake the floor, and Ryan flinched. *Now I'm really out of options...* He glanced back down to the ground below. *Unless...*

He uncurled the amulet's chain from around his

fingers, and took one last look at the artifact's symbols and its deep-red jewel. New resolve coursed through his veins, steeling his nerves.

"Fine, you know what? You want it so bad"--the boy raised the talisman high--"you can have it!" He slammed the object down, onto the hard floor. As the amulet struck the ground its gem shattered, and a shockwave of red light blasted through the room. The force knocked Ryan and Steve onto their backs and rocked the building, its walls creaking and groaning. Ryan grasped the wood around him as best he could and prayed he wouldn't be thrown from the edge.

When the structure finally stood still, Ryan opened his eyes. He climbed to his feet with wobbly legs, while Steve rose into a kneeling position and grabbed the gun up off the floor.

The man's jaw dropped as he stared down at the shards of what once made the amulet's jewel. Though fragmented, it still glowed faintly. "No," he whispered, crawling toward the broken talisman. He sifted through its many pieces. As he touched the shards, the light emanating from them began to fade.

"No," the man said again, louder this time, his voice trembling. "No, no, no. *No!*" He fumbled with the pieces as if to try and put them back together, but it was no use. Their glow faded away completely.

Ryan hadn't been sure the artifact would break, but it had been a gamble worth taking. There was no denying it now; it was utterly destroyed, and dread simmered in his stomach. What did this mean for him? For Boss?

"Do you have any idea what you've done?" Steve asked. The man glowered at the boy, climbing to his feet. "Now you two are stuck this way. Forever."

Guess I've got my answer, Ryan thought, then shrugged. "Oh, well. Better Boss be with me than with you."

Steve's expression fell blank. He raised his colt. "You're gonna wish you were never born."

Ryan closed his eyes. *At least I put up a fight this time...*

Steve cried out suddenly, and Ryan opened his eyes just in time to see Chyann as the girl swung a rebar pipe straight into the side of Steve's head. The man dropped his gun. It hit the ground with a loud thud, and he crumpled to the floor. As he did so, his hat slipped off his head to reveal the shaggy brown hair beneath.

A surge of relief flooded Ryan's body. *Chy to the rescue again. I swear I'll never complain about her saving me from here on out.*

Chyann extended a hand toward Ryan. "Time to go." He accepted her help, and the pair turned and started running back toward the stairs. However, they only managed to travel through the first doorway and a few feet into the next room before the building began shaking again.

The tremors sent them crashing into the floor, just past this room's first pillar. As they tried to help one another up, a deafening *crack* sounded from every corner of the unfinished building.

"That doesn't sound good," Chyann remarked, her tone laced with fear. As if on cue, the roof above them ruptured and broke from the shift. The rubble tumbled toward them.

The teens clambered out of harm's way, only narrowly avoiding the wreckage as it crashed into the ground. "What's happening?" Chyann cried.

"I think all that released energy is bringin' the building down," Ryan said. "C'mon, we gotta get outta here!" They scrambled to their feet and, just as they were about to make their escape, Ryan looked over his shoulder to see Steve as the man woozily stood as well.

The man raised his gun toward them with an unsteady hand. Blood trickled from an open wound on the side of his head. "Don't think for one second that you can just run away from--"

Before Steve Helsing could finish his sentence, a few of the planks beneath him caved in and trapped his right leg. He struggled, trying to climb free, but the rest of the flooring around him cracked apart too. He clawed at the boards and screamed, but it was no use. The man disappeared from the boy's sight, plummeting toward the levels below.

Ryan stared at the hole left in Steve's wake. Anxiety rose in the boy's chest. *Is he finally gone?*

Chyann tugged Ryan's arm. "Forget about that guy! We need to go, remember?" The planks surrounding the pair groaned and creaked and cracked, and Chyann tossed the rebar aside as the teens sprinted toward the stairs.

Ryan led them down two fracturing flights. When they started down their third, a dark shape appeared in the stairwell before them.

"What the hell is goin' on, you guys?" Willy asked, gasping for air. "Is the whole damn building fallin' apart?"

Dust rained over their heads. Ryan yanked Chyann out of the staircase, Willy close behind. The stairway above them crashed down with a thunderous *boom* and a storm of debris, destroying their path of escape as it slammed through two more levels and into the bottom floor. Dust rose toward them from below, and Chyann squeezed Ryan's hand tight.

Willy grimaced at the rubble before them. "Guess that answers my question."

"Any idea what to do now?" Chyann asked.

"I'm workin' on it," Ryan replied. *Okay, we're on the third floor*, he thought. *So unless there are more stairs somewhere else, we might be…*

He swiveled around to examine the third level as quickly as he could. It didn't look much different than any of the others he'd seen thus far, aside from some spare tools and workbenches sitting around. He spotted a massive square opening, probably for a window of sorts, about twenty feet or so to their far left. The wall around it cracked in time with the rest of the building. "This way! Come on!"

They ran across the room, to the opening, and looked out. Below them sat a large dump truck, its bed filled to the brim with dirt. Chyann squeezed Ryan's hand tighter. "No, no. That's too high!"

"Got any better ideas?" Ryan asked.

A roar sounded from above. They turned. A chunk of rubble came crashing down, some of the debris only missing them by inches.

"Fine!" Chyann shouted. Willy took her other hand in his, and the trio glanced briefly at one other.

Willy smiled. "All for one, right?"

Ryan and Chyann nodded. "And one for all," the two said in unison, and they leapt through the opening.

A scream erupted from Ryan's throat, his stomach lurching as they hurtled down. Despite having jumped of his own accord, panic still coursed through his veins. All the while, Chyann yelled as well, and Willy cheered.

They plunged into the bed of the truck. Although they'd landed in soft dirt, the impact still sent waves of pain through Ryan's legs. Regardless, he and his friends wasted no time. They rolled out of the bed and onto the pavement, then sprinted away as more of the building crumbled behind.

Once Ryan figured they'd run far enough so as to not get hurt any more than they already had today, he stopped to look back. As the construction collapsed, its metal, concrete, and wood crushed equipment and vehicles that stood in its path, a sound like a handful of detonated grenades thundering through the air.

After what felt like forever, the rubble settled. Dust swirled around and burned Ryan's throat as he inhaled. He coughed and waved away the particles.

"Holy crap…" Chyann whispered.

"Talk about bringin' down the house," Willy remarked.

Ryan turned toward them and offered the biggest smile of relief he could manage. "We did it," he said, his heart thumping so hard in his chest he wondered if they could hear it. "We actually did it."

"Yes, we did," Chyann began, "And now you owe us one heck of a catch-up."

Ryan lifted a sleeve to his mouth to keep his lungs dirt free. "I'll explain later. For now, we better beat it before somebody shows up."

He turned to leave. Thankfully they'd managed to make it out of there without any major injuries, but sticking around much longer would press their good luck. There was no doubt in his mind that at least a few people had witnessed the building fall, and if that was the case the sheriff would already be on his way.

"Before we go," Chyann continued, "Where did you hide that body, Will? We need to take it with us."

Ryan tilted his head to the side, unsure he'd heard that correctly. After all, the dust was so thick he could barely see his friends. That could probably affect your hearing too, right?

"Oh, yeah," Willy said. "It's over by the gate we came through."

Okay, so I did hear correctly, Ryan thought as he followed them in the general direction of the gate they'd squeezed past earlier. *Guess they had a whole plan behind the scenes that I didn't know about.*

The scent of the corpse, the putrid smell of death, reached Ryan's nostrils long before he caught sight of the remains. *Probably for the best that we don't leave Boss's body lying around for people to find, anyway...* Thankfully there were plenty of back alleys and paths they could take home that would avoid prying eyes. Ryan wasn't looking forward to carrying the remains all that way, though.

Soon they left the construction yard with Boss's body in tow, grime blurring the sight of the wreckage behind.

EPILOGUE

Late afternoon sun warmed Ryan's backyard as he stood beneath the tall thin oak tree rooted at its rear. The tree had stood here for as long as he could remember, although it always appeared to be dead or dying. Its bark was darker than that of healthy oaks, and its many limbs only ever held a handful of leaves.

Thick pine bushes lined Ryan's fence, hiding what he was about to do from his neighbors (not that they snooped much, anyway). Between him and the old tree sat an open grave that he'd dug into the healthy green grass of the yard, and inside of the shallow hole Boss's sheet-covered corpse lay.

The Ooawan's ghostly visage hovered over the left half of Ryan's face as the pair stared down at the body. The scent emanating from it was beginning to take up permanent residence in Ryan's nostrils, and it took constant effort to keep himself from gagging in its cloud.

Ryan glanced over to the can of gasoline beside him, then at the lawn's hose head, turned on and ready to go. Disposing of dead bodies wasn't something he had experience with, but Boss had insisted on doing so like this, and he wasn't about to take the chance of burning his house down in the process.

He shifted his gaze to a book of matches in his hand; in the other he held a bag. Ryan raised the sack and gave it a shake. "Is this everything?"

"Everything I had on me," Boss confirmed. Ryan nodded as he returned his attention to the gasoline can. Doubt swarmed his mind the longer he thought about what they were preparing to do.

"Are you sure about this?" he asked.

"Yes, I'm sure."

Ryan set the bag down and grabbed the gas can. He unscrewed the cap, then poured the liquid over the Ooawan's remains.

"Without the amulet, I can't return to my body." Boss furrowed his brow. "At least this way I'm getting something the rest of my kind did not."

Ryan scrunched his nose. "What's that?"

"A proper burial." Boss's voice was laced with sorrow, and Ryan fell quiet. He wasn't sure how to respond to that, wasn't sure how he could comfort the Ooawan.

The boy dropped the can once it was empty. He ripped the book of matches, lighting the entire pack, and tossed them into the grave. The corpse caught fire immediately. An uneasy hush settled between the pair as they watched the flames flicker and dance above what was once Montra Bos.

Of course, the blaze did nothing to help the smell. It shifted from a scent reminiscent of spoiled meat into something more like wet fur mixed with rotten barbecue. He couldn't say it smelled worse now, but it was a far cry from smelling better.

A long while passed, and Ryan decided to grab up the bag again and open it. And, as he scanned its contents, his stomach dropped. *Boss's dagger.*

He pulled out the weapon to examine it. The stone blade had been carved on all sides into a fine, razor-sharp edge and was tied to a pristine white bone. It reminded him of an arrowhead he'd received in elementary school while learning about the Indigenous peoples of the United States, and he shook the tool to test its sturdiness. No wobbling, no looseness. Clearly it had been well-crafted.

Steve Helsing's words haunted his memories, bringing with them seeds of doubt. "*He wasn't being peaceful when he drove his dagger into my sleeping brother's back.*" The thought sent chills down Ryan's spine.

"What is it?" Boss asked, and Ryan flinched at the question, surprised the Ooawan hadn't sensed his worries already. *We must still have some separate thoughts when we aren't talking to each other.*

"Nothing," Ryan answered. "Just didn't get to see this up close until now." Boss didn't seem convinced by this answer but didn't press further, and Ryan stuffed the weapon back into the bag and reached for another item: a key.

The old thing appeared to be made of iron. Its lower half had been molded into some strange symbol, almost like a peace sign, although if it had been a peace sign once it looked as if someone had squeezed the sides until it had become an oval instead of a circle.

Ryan turned the key in his hand. "What's this for?"

"I don't know," Boss said. "It was given to me by Magnus before we parted ways."

Ryan stared hard at the item, finding it difficult to ignore the strong sense of familiarity he felt with it. It was like when you'd seen the same car every day at the same time for weeks, but if someone asked for the vehicle's make or model, you wouldn't be able to tell them anything about it aside from the color.

"I've seen this symbol somewhere before..." He slid it into his pocket rather than inside the bag with the rest of Boss's things, then returned to watching the flames. "Look, Boss... I, uhhh... I'm sorry."

"You have nothing to be sorry for."

"Yeah, I do. You helped me out back at school, and I flipped. I almost got us killed by Steve, I smashed the amulet..." He nodded with a guilty smile before continuing. "Can't help but feel a bit responsible for that one since it was kind of our only way to... y'know."

"Get me to not be riding shotgun?"

Ryan chuckled. "Yeah, exactly. Look, we might be stuck this way for a while, so we should probably learn to get along."

"Aye, it won't do either of us good to be fighting. I still don't understand why you're willing to help me so much. You put your life on the line against Helsing."

The boy bowed his head. "To tell you the truth, I didn't know what to do. I just kinda tried to think about what my grandpa would have done if he were here. And he helped you before, so… yeah." A familiar sadness made his chest tighten. "Since he's gone, I guess that makes you my problem now." Boss didn't offer a response, and silence enveloped the two.

Finally, the fire began to die down ever so slightly, and Ryan kicked some dirt into the grave. "We should probably start filling this hole in before the whole neighborhood starts to smell like burnt fur." He reached over to grab the shovel.

"Your friends…" Boss started, and Ryan paused. "You were right about them. They stood by us both, regardless of everything. I may not trust them myself, but I do trust you."

Ryan smiled a little as he stabbed the shovel into the mound of dirt next to them, then dumped the earth into Boss's grave. He did this again and again until the ground was even, snuffing out the flames and burying the corpse.

Chyann and Willy sat in Ryan's living room as the TV before them played an old black and white sci-fi show. The narrator closed out the episode, the title *Shadow Falls* appearing through a floating door while the rerun came to an end.

Chyann wasn't sure what the episode had been about. Between her thoughts of what had happened to them earlier that day and Willy's nonstop chatter about it, she hadn't paid much attention.

"I'm just sayin' Chy," Willy exclaimed. "It was awesome! We were like a bunch of action movie stars or something!"

Chyann snatched the remote and changed the channel to an old sitcom on the comedy network, trying not to roll her eyes. Clearly she and Will had very different opinions regarding today's events. "Are you forgetting that we almost died?"

Willy pumped a fist into the air. "You bet your ass I am!"

She shook her head. Despite how heavily she disagreed with his sentiments, she couldn't help but chuckle at how much the situation had fired him up. He was funny that way. He was also a real pain in the ass, and a huge jerk sometimes, but she couldn't help loving him all the same.

Before she could shut down his suggestions for them to find another building in town to destroy, the glass door leading into the backyard slammed shut, and they turned to see Ryan as he approached them.

"Hey," Chyann said. She could see from the way Ryan slumped his shoulders that he was uncomfortable. They never kept secrets from each other, but considering how wild his undisclosed info was, she didn't exactly blame him for keeping it from her.

Willy spun around in his seat to face Ryan, and the boy smiled nervously, his gaze darting from side to side.

"All good out there?" Willy asked.

"Burned and buried," Ryan replied with a nod. "Now that we've got some down time, I…" He trailed off, then took a deep breath before finally meeting their gazes and continuing, "No, we. *We* have something to tell you guys."

The cat creature that Chyann had gathered was named Boss appeared once again, the ghostly left half of his face overtaking Ryan's. The sight sent her head reeling. *What, or who, is this thing?* Her mind demanded answers ever since she had first seen this phenomenon behind the school earlier that day. Now, right here in Ryan's living room, she was about to get the answers she wanted.

She and Willy sat, ready to listen to the tale, and Ryan and Boss began, starting with the early morning outside of Twilight Peak, Wyoming two days ago.

Something had happened. Legacy wasn't sure what, but he knew something was different. Supernatural beings had been drawn to Twilight Peak for years, coming here from all over. Monsters, demons, wicked entities, anything mobile enough to find its way.

This, however, was entirely new, an ancient evil that made the hairs on his arms stand on end even underneath his thick robe. For the first time in over thirty years, he was *afraid*. He hated this feeling.

Normally he knew what kind of vile things prowled about out there, and that knowledge made him brave. Knowing, as we are all aware, is half the battle.

But this evil, whatever it was, seemed to be something not even he recognized. Even after all this time, after all this information on the hidden world had been collected, not a single document or slip of paper recorded anything closely resembling what this foul thing might be.

Legacy sat in a room containing reports such as these, where every single secret and hidden evil inhabiting the state of Wyoming had been categorized on the shelves mere feet away from him. The area wasn't incredibly big, but it had enough space for everything sorted, so it being cramped didn't bother him.

Whatever has come has something to do with those three, he thought. *But why?* After all, they had always been here. What changed? In time, he suspected he would find out. Nothing stayed hidden forever.

Nothing except for him, of course.

A familiar and masculine voice asked from behind, "Do you think it's something we need to worry about?" Legacy turned to see Heritage enter the room, his clean white robe illuminated in the dim light coming from the bulb above. He'd pulled his hood low over his head, a large black eye stitched on top--the same symbol many generations before them had used as well. "What if they become a problem down the road?"

Legacy wasn't sure what to tell his companion. After all, these things needed to be handled delicately. Obviously they were a part of this new and unknown evil somehow, but a problem? He opened a dark folder and rested it on his table, next to the loose polaroid photos a Follower had taken earlier that day, before turning back to Heritage. "No. In fact, I believe they could be of use."

"How so, sir?"

"They're our only lead on whatever has found its way to Twilight Peak."

"Another entity has come searching for the tomb, you think?"

That didn't sound right to Legacy, but he didn't have any reason to believe otherwise. The tomb continued to elude him and the Eye as one of the last great mysteries of Twilight Peak. It made him uneasy, but he had confidence it would be uncovered. Almost every stone in this town had been turned. Most secrets had been discovered. If the people here knew what was hidden deep within that tomb…

But that didn't matter now. What mattered were these three children, and he wouldn't stop until he knew what had taken such an interest in them. Only a matter of time.

"It's possible." He slid the last photo into his folder. It joined a plethora of others, all taken within the past day. "For now," he continued, "Put a watch on each of these people at all times. I want to know what their connection is."

"I will put an order out immediately. May I have their names once more?"

Legacy closed the folder, revealing a white eye spray-painted onto the front, similar to the symbols decorating their robes. He slipped the folder under his arm, then turned to Heritage. "Ryan Myers, Chyann Wakeman, and William Wylee. Find out what you can about that man who died in the building as well."

Heritage bowed. "Of course, sir."

"Besides, if they *do* become a problem, we have Genesis on standby. He would be delighted to deal with any issues that may arise."

Legacy jerked his head at a third figure in the room, the one who leaned against the closest wall. Tall and wide, Genesis had adjusted his hood in matching fashion to Heritage's, though his robe was ashen black rather than white, and he had a matching gas mask of custom design strapped over his face, concealing his features.

Having Genesis around always comforted Legacy. He was, after all, the greatest killer among their ranks.

"Of course, sir," Heritage repeated, then exited the chamber. Even after Heritage disappeared, Genesis said nothing. Instead he stood silently, ready to accept his orders.

Legacy strode a few steps to the nearest shelf and slid the folder into an empty space. "We'll be keeping a very close eye on our new friends," he said, and it wasn't hard to do so. Not for him. "Come, Genesis. In the meantime, I have a task for you."

Genesis straightened and sauntered toward the doorway. Before following, Legacy reached up and pulled on an overhanging cord, casting the room into complete darkness.

WRITTEN BY
D.R. MILLS

TO BE CONTINUED
IN BOOK 2

THE GIRL NEXT DOOR

*If you would like to follow D. R. Mills's journey or the **MONSTERS** series specifically, check out the author's official Twitter and Instagram accounts:*

- Instagram: @monsters_bookseries

- Twitter: @MonstersSeries

- Facebook: @Monsters/100067554032850

- TikTok: www.tiktok.com/@monstersseries

If you enjoyed the story, dont forget to leave a review on your preferred platform! Reviews help authors find more readers, and if you'd like D. R. Mills to be able to release books faster, reviews are the best way to support him.

ACKNOWLEDGMENTS

This very first book was a long time coming, and many years have been dedicated to the story, not just in this particular book, but overall. As such, it never would have made it this far without the help of some amazing people, so I'd like to take a moment to give them the credit they deserve.

First and foremost, I'd like to give a special thanks to my beautiful wife, *Emily*, who gave me the time and space to be able to work on all of this, the never ending support behind my passion, and for being a great help when I needed to bounce some ideas. Thank you for everything, my love. There's absolutely nobody else like you, and you've done more for me and this book than you'll ever know.

Next, I'd like to thank my writing buddy, the amazing *A. P. Mobley*, whose experience, advice, ideas, and just general help were essential in getting this book made. I'm almost certain that you would not be reading it now if not for her. She's taught me a lot, and I'm looking forward to learning more as I progress. Seriously Ali, thank you for all your hard work. I hope you're just as proud of this book as I am, and I can't wait to see what the future holds for you!

A special thanks to the seriously talented *Gabrielle Ragusi* is in order as well. She's done all the official art for both **MONSTERS**, as well as the other series in the

Sea of Ink family. Her work is beautiful, and I can't imagine anyone else bringing my characters to life the way she has. I hope you all look through more of her work and give it the attention it deserves. Thank you so much for everything you've made for me thus far, Gabrielle. I sincerely hope you enjoy working with me as much as I enjoy working with you!

And of course, my very own mother deserves a shout out as well. She's inspired me greatly my entire life, and supported me wholeheartedly no matter what my passions have been. There's really no way I could ever repay her for everything she's done. I love you, mom! You deserve the world and I wish I could give it to you. Writing a book is close enough, right?

The team over at Enchanted Ink Publishing deserve a special thanks for being able to help me put this book together last minute, and although I haven't seen what they've done for me at the time of writing this, I know I'm in good hands. Thank you for being so professional and easy to work with!

I'd also like to give a quick thank you to *Jenna Moreci* for all her writing videos on YouTube. They really gave me a good idea on what I was doing right and what I was doing wrong, so thank you for putting that advice out there for newbies like me who needed it.

There are countless other friends and family that had a hand, however small, in my journey to this point.

Crutches: For all the *(REALLY OLD)* beta reading you did for my *(REALLY OLD)* early work. You're a big reason I stuck with this for so long. Please never forget how grateful I am for all your support.

Cole: For being the chillest homie and stickin' by me all these years. We may not always have time to talk or hang out, but know I'm thinking about you every day, brother. I'm glad you're in a good place in your life right now!

J-MAN: For giving me brutally honest feedback. Thank you for not being afraid to tell me when my ideas suck. It may hurt my feelings sometimes, but I need that kind of feedback to make my stories the absolute best they can be.

Lastly, I'd like to thank you, the reader. Thank you for giving **MONSTERS** a chance. I really hope you'll stick by Ryan and the others as they move forward. There's more to come, and I'm already hard at work on the next few books for your enjoyment. I'm not sure when that may be, but I'm really hoping sooner rather than later. I'll be sure to post some regular updates as I go!

Until then,
--DRM

D. R. MILLS

is a young-adult horror author who is currently hard at work on his debut series, *MONSTERS*. He was born and raised in Wyoming, where he's still lurking around somewhere. When he isn't writing, he's playing video games a borderline unhealthy amount or spending time with his beautiful wife.

WWW.SEAOFINKPRESS.WORDPRESS.COM